THE
BLACK CLOVER
BOOK

Liminal Books

The Black Clover book is a work of fiction. Names, characters, places, and incidents are the product of the author's imagination or are used fictitiously. Any resemblance to actual events, locales, or persons, living or dead, is coincidental.

Liminal Books is an imprint of Between the Lines Publishing. The Liminal Books name and logo are trademarks of Between the Lines Publishing.

Copyright © 2024 by Whitney Poole

Cover Artwork: Kamilla Sims

Cover Design: Morgan Bliadd

Between the Lines Publishing and its imprints supports the right to free expression and the value of copyright. The scanning, uploading, and distribution of this book without permission is a theft of the author's intellectual property. If you would like permission to use material from the book (other than for review purposes), please contact info@btwnthelines.com.

Between the Lines Publishing
1769 Lexington Ave N, Ste 286
Roseville MN 55113
btwnthelines.com

First Published: September 2024

ISBN: Paperback 978-1-958901-92-2

ISBN: Ebook 978-1-958901-93-9

Library of Congress Cataloging-in-Publication Data

Identifiers: LCCN 2024026429 (print) | LCCN 2024026430 (ebook) | ISBN 9781958901922 (trade paperback) | ISBN 9781958901939 (ebook)
Subjects: LCGFT: Science fiction. | Novels. Classification: LCC PS3616.O638 B57 2024 (print) | LCC PS3616.O638 (ebook) | DDC 813/.6--dc23/eng/20240724 LC record available at https://lccn.loc.gov/2024026429 LC ebook record available at https://lccn.loc.gov/2024026430

The publisher is not responsible for websites (or their content) that are not owned by the publisher.

THE
BLACK CLOVER
BOOK

Whitney Poole

One

I leave this writing as a record of simpler times, times that did not know they were harbingers of a new way of living. There was talk during these days of separation. Those who whispered in the dimly lit alleys and clubs would become my co-conspirators as events overtook me, carrying me with the zeitgeist of a city turned upside-down. My family and I would persevere and forge bonds with my newfound fellows, all because of a new way of thinking that would become the new mode of living. This was the legacy of the Black Clover. My name is Freddie Freeman, and I am one of the Black Clover now.

Monolith City was all I had known. From Maxwell's Hanging Gardens to King's Cradle, the Grand Coliseum to Quincy Square, and even to where I lived in the Atlas, Monolith City brimmed with tribute to how we survived since the Great Migration. A time when everyone had become uprooted due to climate change and there were great wanderings. No one knew stability until the monolith appeared. It showed us where to settle and how to build our city. Since that time, each mayor dedicated a monument to the city that had sprung up and Mayor Oaks had another underway.

Oaks was up for Mayor again and as usual, he was running on a unity campaign. However, all that really meant was that if you disagreed with him, you disappeared. Years ago, back when people still believed in elections, my mother became one of the missing.

I had a comfortable life as a journalist at the beginning of his service. I still had faith in the written word then. I began to cover Oaks at the Monolith Sentinel, covering his civil rights abuses in search of a cleaner city.

My father and I lived in the Atlas district. It was built not far from The Hill, on which the capital stood. Full of rowhouses, the Atlas was a community of diversity. Church goers mingled with street performers, who mingled with farmers selling locally grown produce. Murals greeted visitors, telling them where we—the Atlas—had come from.

Oaks was running for reelection. Instead of the bright-eyed zeal and optimism that should greet a citizen in the morning, I awoke in quite a different fashion. I had fallen into a deep sleep with dreams of being reunited with my mother. Sadly, I was yanked from that comfort by the curious sensation of wet pants. My bed was soaked, and I felt nauseous as my room seemed to move. The walls ambled around me, shifting heights. My nightstand and lamp floated in and out of reach. I removed my feet from the sodden mess of blankets. I tried to place my feet firmly on the wooden floor but plunged waist deep into a flow of glacial water. The first floor of my house had flooded.

My dresser and nightstand were afloat. Their wooden tops wobbled dumbly about my bedroom. I pulled my grandmother's saturated quilt from where it was still wrapped around me and tossed it aside with a heavy splash. Icy droplets peppered my face, and they sent another shiver cascading through me. I realized I could no longer stay in my house. The tall slender neck and shade of my lamp floated away from me through the door. One of the fish from my aquarium swam past. I waded slowly through what once was my hallway, now a river, from the bedroom to the study. The walls echoed with the sound of water lapping. In my study, half of my notebooks were underwater. So much thought lost. A creeping pool of ink flowed from them, as if an octopus had been threatened. I opened my window and immediately regretted my decision as it was the inauguration of the exodus of my belongings from my house.

I was thrown up against the sill in the deluge. My belongings attacked me one after another. I fended off the lamp with my forearms. Several books got in a few good blows before rebounding off my torso out the window. The entire affair unnerved me. I took my sopping quilt, which had tangled itself around me like seaweed and threw it off, glowering at my fish who looked quite happy jumping out the window.

I leaned my head outside and found the entire street was flooded.

Directly across from me, a woman was washing her laundry in the flood waters. Her children were taking the clothes she scrubbed and hanging them from the sill on the side of the house, where they looked like flags that fluttered in the breeze.

A few people gathered by the windows to watch the flood, but most acted as if it was any other day. Some men were barbecuing steaks on a balcony nearby.

I thought to check on Dad. He was no stranger to waking up incontinent, but I thought a full-on flood would merit some attention on my part. I waded through the waist deep water toward his bedroom.

I shouted up at him, "Dad, are you okay?"

He hollered back, "I'm trying to sleep!"

Out front, water covered the whole street. I could see the tops of mailboxes and cars. On the street of water from my window, I saw a skiff captained by a man who stopped periodically at windows to collect what appeared to be bottles. He took them from people watching television in their homes. They passed him the clear, plastic bottles that reflected the sunlight and thanked him. People would call down from the high levels and drop bottles as well. The captain added them to a pile he had on the bottom of the boat.

I called out to him. "What are you doing?"

He motored across the street of water to my window. "Collecting votes," he said. "It's election day." He pointed with his hand to a white sheet hung from the front of the boat. It read 'Mobile Voting Station' in black, spray-painted letters. "The voting station at the school is underwater. I said we have to collect votes somehow. The people of the Atlas need a voice. I took to the streets to collect votes from people's homes. All you have to do is write your name and address on one side of a sheet of paper, your election choices on the other, and seal it in a bottle." He smiled warmly at me.

"Why the bottle," I asked.

"So, the votes don't get wet, of course."

I took a bottle and a sheet of paper and cast my ballot.

"Thank you for your civic pride," he said and took off to the next building.

Some streets were sandbagged. At several houses, shelters were raised on roofs. People simply kept climbing up, utilizing all manner of conveyance and execution to stay ahead of the rising water. And still, throughout the city, people acted as if nothing happened. It was a collective ignorance of the state of affairs in the city.

"Some day we're having." It was shouted from above.

I looked up and Dad waved at me from the roof.

"Yes, some day." I answered angrily.

I crawled out onto my sill from the frigid water in my house. Bud, my neighbor, threw a rope and told me to climb up. I grabbed hold of the rope and swung over to his house. I pulled myself along as quickly as I could until I could clamber over the edge of the roof. I stood shivering in the cold and surveyed the landscape with disbelieving eyes.

The whole of the neighborhood was underwater. What once was a grid of streets was now a network of canals. The tops of houses were all I could see. It was as if the entire neighborhood had been cut in half. Instead of people walking the streets, small boats navigated the canals. Men and women congregated on rooftops as if they were patios. The water sparkled in the morning light.

I gasped at the sight. "What is this?"

"Every so often something breaks. Mains, generators, beams. Keeps life exciting, you know?" Bud grinned at me.

"You'd think that the city would be more prepared."

"Prepared? Of course, they're prepared. What do you think they're doing? Eating turkey sandwiches? Look, there are some people from the Department of Public Works over there." He pointed to the canal. Further up the current, I saw a small rowboat into which four men were crammed. One stood on the bow, a megaphone in hand. Pieces of his announcements told everyone to stay calm, keep their eyes open, go back to their everyday lives. I pieced together that some sort of taskforce was being formed to look into the matter. Two others manned the oars. The fourth sat in the back with a silver counting machine held in his hand. Every so often he took note of something in one of the houses and added another tick to his count.

As they drew closer, I noticed that the boat was spinning in circles. The oarsmen were rowing in opposite directions. At first, I thought it was intentional so that the announcements would reach everyone on the roofs. Then I saw them stop and argue over which way they were headed. After a few heated words they both raised their oars and began rowing in the other direction so that now they spun counter to their previous course.

My belongings were slowly becoming scattered about the neighborhood by the current. There was little chance I would find them, or if I did, that they would be in a usable state. I had difficulty combining a place of ideals with the absurdity in which I found myself. I saw in the officials, a chance for explanation.

"What is the explanation for this?" I demanded of the man with the megaphone.

As he spun in lazy, advancing circles below me, he lowered his megaphone.

"It was amazing. There was a break in the reservoir. You should have heard the crack. I heard it from a half-mile away. Still can't get it out of my ears. Water gushed out from the broken locks right into the streets. All the drains are clogged with caulk for some strange reason, so all the water had no place else to go. Since the houses here are attached, they're perfect for canals."

The implausibility of his words irked me. "You can't expect me to believe this was caused by some caulk and cracks. Look, you can see my furniture being swept out of my house as we speak." The water level had risen, and with it, my dresser and nightstand had floated out of the house. They looked forgotten, like the cargo of a sinking ship. One oar caught in the floe of furniture accumulating in the canal. The oarsman began hacking at an end table fiercely, trying to fend it away. The movement upset the balance of the boat, causing it to rock dangerously. The man with the megaphone scrambled for his balance. By now the boat had begun to pass. I ran to the edge of Bud's roof, shouting at them.

"You don't have any other explanation?"

He answered me in shouts as the boat drifted. "The Department of Public Works is not responsible. This flood is an act inorganic soleck, solecs." The "c" caught in his throat each time he tried to say the word. He consulted the man with the ticker. "How do I say it?"

"Inorganic solecism. Three S's."

"Right. Inorganic solecism. No fault of ours."

"Inorganic solecism? What does that mean?"

He yelled back at me. "There are dictionaries at the City Archives! I suggest you look there!"

He raised the megaphone to his mouth and began to recite the same phrases from earlier. The sound dwindled out of earshot as the four of them floated down the canal spinning in one direction, then another.

"Don't worry," I assured Dad. "The water will recede in a couple of hours." I doubted my own words, but I had to say something. I said this as much to calm myself as Dad.

Our houses formed rows of shoals that dotted the valley. Some rows had built bridges to span the canals. People walked back and forth freely conducting the shopping and visits they would otherwise. Except now, they went from roof to roof instead of house to house. The main entrance of every house was now the attic window. All of the transactions of the day still occurred on our rooftop city in the sea. Canoes and rafts slowly navigated the canals. An occasional skiff drove past, the hum of its engine echoing along the roofs.

Bud had retrieved a fishing pole from somewhere and was casting off the other side of the roof. Our row was still isolated, though I suppose I could have hailed a canoe. I sat down next to him. A child splashed his legs across the canal from me.

"Any idea what inorganic solecism means?"

"Is that a fish?

There was an old man passing by on a raft. He and his wife had set a table precariously in between them. On it were several plates and glasses of wine.

I cupped my hands and yelled at the man in the raft. "Excuse me! Excuse me! Hey! Do you know what inorganic solecism means?"

"Yes! It means we're fucked!" He smiled back and waved at me.

"What?"

"Fucked! Nothing we can do!"

His demeanor was still jovial. "How can you smile at that?" I asked.

"It's my anniversary. The wife and I are celebrating just like we did thirty years ago!"

"There was a flood thirty years ago?"

"No! But we celebrated all the same!"

"Don't you think there should be an alternative?"

"Eh?" The raft was drifting out of earshot.

"Don't you think there should be an alternative?" I shouted.

His wife tugged at his shoulder and shouted into his ear. "He said, 'Don't you think there should be an alternative?'"

"An alternative to what?" he yelled.

"Inorganic solecism!"

"Oh." He looked as if someone had told him people lived on the moon.

"Sure! But what can you do?" He shrugged this last comment and returned to the oars. As the raft moved down the canal, he sang to her. His wife blushed at the back of the raft. She giggled, covering her mouth with a flash of modesty.

They continued talking loudly, probably due to his deafness, as they drifted.

"Such a nice young man." She said as she waved goodbye.

"Eh?"

"Such a nice young man!"

He muttered a last barely audible statement. "Why does such a nice young man always have to ruin dinner for me?"

I knew the mayoral race would be tight, and I would find that when every other district checked in, Mayor Oaks led by a few votes. The people of the Atlas could have turned the tide, yet no one knew how the Atlas had voted. No one was sure what had happened. All we knew was that inorganic solecism was to blame.

My conspirators and I would leave behind the shackles of our past for a new consciousness that had evolved from the budding petals of our tumultuous times. I am getting ahead of myself though, for this came later. All I can say is that there was unrest, and a growing number of people sympathized with a desire for something new. It was out of this newness that the flood came one morning. It was a shock to all, at least those that could recognize it.

Two

Trace doses of quiet remained from that day.

I found my dictionary; sodden and wrinkled by water. The pages nearly tore as I flipped back and forth between two definitions, trying to piece together some sort of meaning for the phrase 'inorganic solecism.' I've consulted many different dictionaries since then. From those books, I've constructed several meanings, none of which are very plausible. The most likely of my constructions is as follows: a systematic breach resulting from a cause not due to the creator, user, or bystander of said system. I doubt there is such a thing.

I am an antiquarian. I relish reading documents from before the Great Migration. It was said we went from kings to slaves to kings once again. So much time was spent traveling. Our songs and stories speak of the struggles we endured. Everyone had to make sacrifices and so much was lost. We broke, then remolded, society into an image of what we had known. How familiar it would be to our ancestors remains a mystery. That is why I cherish what texts I have. We had finally found a place that felt like home. Monolith City stood as a beacon for what we could be. The Atlas was its jewel.

The neighbors on the adjoining roof agreed to keep an eye on my dad as I left the Atlas to see what measures were being taken to help us. Outside my house there was all kinds of flotsam. Cars, wooden planks, and vegetation all floated passed. I spied a man on a raft. He sold kayaks. I swam out and purchased one from him. He said, "It ain't like last time." Curious words from a curious fellow. Still, his presence was fortuitous. Without him, I would not have been able to see the rest of the city. The kayak would carry me out of the Atlas to the Hill.

Streets, like arteries, filled with water and ran through the city. They pulsed with life, each globule moving swiftly with the current dragging debris. I navigated the tops of buildings jutting out of the flood with great concern. So many buildings underwater…how could anything function? I dipped my paddle into the waters of the flood. The current picked up as I approached a corner where two flows of water connected. In the center, the triangular roof of a museum jutted out. Finger-like branches of trees surrounded the museum. I aligned my kayak with the current and rode into the broad expanse of floodwater. If this were a network of veins, the park with the Baldwin Building underneath would be the vena cava. Here many routes met and pulsed with a life hard to resist. On the roof, several men stood. Some sat near the edge, dipping their feet into the water; the cuffs of their jeans rolled up, looking like they were on vacation.

One man grasped a limb and swung onto a tree, climbing until he had a reached a central spot at the top of it. Other men were harassing someone. From the rooftop where they were stranded, they hooted and jeered at a man in a boat.

"How does it feel to be mayor?"

"Why don't you answer him, Oaksey?"

"We're all stuck here. What you gonna do about it?"

"Yeah, where's my piece of the stimulus?"

The pursued retorted, "Show some respect."

It was Mayor Oaks.

I began paddling faster, hoping to catch him. He caught sight of me over his shoulder and redoubled his efforts, paddling twice on each side before switching. My kayak was nimbler than his canoe, but he had launched himself into a swift current. I battled against the eddies near the shore, trying to get closer, as I hurled my questions at him from behind.

I used my paddle to turn and found the branches of a large tree standing in my path. I tried to dodge them, but my kayak became caught in the limbs. Oaks took off at this point. He hastened his trek to the Tubman House, where he worked while I was stuck untangling myself from the top of a submerged tree.

It would seem my questions had to wait.

I became a journalist because of lost tradition. The establishments we had were copied from a previous way of living. Some worked. Most didn't. We pieced together as best we could, from what was remembered of our past. The monolith showed us how to live, but it too became forgotten. I clung to journalism with a hope for what could be; a hope for the truth in our daily affairs. My mother felt the same way. She disappeared because of her beliefs.

At the Monolith Sentinel newspaper office where I worked, a trip which took me quite a while to make, I asked around to see if anyone else had trouble with the flood.

"What flood?" said Jones.

"The one in the Atlas. I had to kayak here this morning."

"Nothing on social media about a flood. Must be your imagination."

I held up my leg. "I'm dripping wet. How do you think that happened?"

"Incontinence?" Garcia asked.

The editor-in-chief walked by. "Chief, what have you heard about a flood?" I asked.

The chief wore a blue button-down and suspenders. He wiped sweat from his furrowed forehead. "What a disaster. Election day has come and we're all the better for it."

Jones spoke up. "What are you talking about, chief? It's going to be a contested election. Not all the districts can weigh in."

I chimed in. "There's a flood in the Atlas. No one can vote. The whole district is in an uproar. Why haven't we covered this?"

"Elections are formalities. They are easily fixed," said the chief.

"Such bald cynicism belongs to Oaks, not the Sentinel," I said. "We're making the same mistakes over again."

This was the first instance where I noticed that I was alone at the Sentinel. No one else believed in the flood. Certainly, my neighbors in the Atlas acknowledged it. They had to. But what about the rest of the city? The flood unnerved me so much that I had forgotten about the election almost entirely.

As I began to ask about Oaks' interference in the election, two lines of hulking men in nondescript gray suits filed in from the entryway. They carried assault rifles and wore black balaclavas over their heads. It was an opposing sight: business from the neck down and militant form the neck up. Their imposing figures fanned out across the newsroom with their backs to the walls facing the journalists. They looked like gorillas with guns.

The chief spoke up. "Ah, right on time. These, uh, gentlemen are part of Oaks' media team. They are here to help with quality assurance as we make the transition to our new format.

"Oaks has everything on lockdown. The Great Firewall, he calls it. No media posts of any kind are allowed unless it meets with the censors' approval. He doesn't want any speech out of line to be heard."

"What about our freedom?" I asked. "This city was built on our ability to speak our minds!"

The editor-in-chief addressed his stable of writers. He held a stack of paper in his hand and placed it down on the desk.

"These are the pieces you're supposed to write.

It came down from on high. Oaks himself has refused to let us cover anything else. These are our talking points. Anything off topic won't make it in the paper. We get a new list each day. Make sure you're on topic."

"Chief, you can't be serious?"

"What if one slips through?" Jones asked.

"There will be penalties for both the paper and the writer if a non-sanctioned article gets published."

I looked over the list. "I'm writing about house and gardens?"

The chief said, "The paper will go down the tubes if we don't shape up. We're lucky to be running a paper in the digital era. The city has guidelines for its coverage as well. You want access? You have to play the game. With pre-recorded sound bits it's a wonder anyone reads at all."

"What happened to our integrity?"

"Everyone's got to work together. Oaks wants us to prove them wrong."

"Who is them?

"The separatists"

I was dumbfounded First the denial by everyone around me of the flood, of which I had evidence and now this – suppression of free speech. "Separatists? Who are they? What about the fourth estate? What about the flood? What about any protest demonstrations being suppressed or those who are jailed without warrants?"

"Off the menu. You can't order off menu."

"Unbelievable. I can't work like this."

"Suit yourself. We can find new talent for less. It's what the higher ups want."

Garcia, a friend of mine whom I collaborated with sometimes, spun a chair in front of him. "Bullshit!"

"What a doozy," Jones said.

Jones and I looked over the menu as the chief looked over the stable of writers. Just at that moment, a commotion came from over by the wall. One of the suited gorillas edged closer to Jones, who was typing notes on the meeting, bumping Jones' chair away from the computer.

"Just what do you think you're doing!" Jones asked.

The member of the media team grunted at Jones. His cohorts lining the walls began to grunt as well. Grunts filled the air of the room with a sonic barrage that clouded thought from anyone's mind.

The chief spoke up. "Now, Jones, we don't want to upset anyone. Just back away from the computer. I guess Oaks doesn't want notes to be taken on his new policies."

Grunts filled the room once more and the gorilla that bumped Jones stepped back to his place at the wall, after Jones settled in a few feet away from the computer.

The chief pulled out a box that he added to the desk. "We're also being ordered to wear these flag pins. It's part of Oak's Pride program. He says that all inhabitants of the city who are truly patriotic citizens should wear them."

"Or else what?"

"Just wear the damn thing. It's easier than complaining."

The pins bore the flag of the city – a black monolith on a yellow circle surrounded by a field of green. I fastened one to my collar.

"Thomas, you live in the Atlas, right? Back me up. There's a flood in the Atlas. This is news."

Thomas wiped his forehead with the sleeve of his shirt. "It's not on the list, boss."

"That's right," the chief said. "If it's not on the list, we don't report it."

"But I saw it myself. My legs are dripping wet."

"Take it up with the mayor, Freddie. He' giving a press conference later today. I want you to cover it. He'll go over the talking points then."

"But the flood... my house..."

"Sorry Freeman, business is business."

I hit the streets in search of someone outside the Atlas who acknowledged the flood.

Since my mother had disappeared, others had joined her. Monolith City was becoming peppered with groups of lost people. For every movement that sprung up in favor of women, labor, and ecology, stitches were torn out of our city. Its sleeves were becoming ragged. Oaks was intimidating his way into an omnipresent office. The only respite I had from the feeling of fright my family endured was the whisper of an organization that would upend his reign – the Black Clover.

One of the guys from the press room ribbed me on the street. "Freeman, your neighborhood can't be flooding. It's not on the list."

"Doesn't anyone care? The city is flooding. Half of it will be underwater by the end of the week!"

"Business as usual. Freeman, we can't get in a huff about every crisis that happens in this city. There's always something - economic recession, murder spree, drug scandal..."

"And now a flood."

"No flood. We've got a job to do. To report. On these talking points of course."

"What's the point of reporting if we can't say what's actually happening in the city?"

"Freddie, you'll get it one day. Job security. You've got to grease the palms that feed you."

My phone buzzed. On the street, everyone was looking down at their phones as well. A piercing alarm came from all our phones. We stared at the electronic devices and watched as a live stream began to broadcast. A pudgy man with a bald head and puffy salt and pepper sideburns stood behind a wooden podium bearing the city's seal – a pillar on which stood an eagle holding laurels. Deep blue curtains were closed behind the man at the podium. It was Oaks. He straightened the knot of his red tie and brushed back his sideburns.

He spoke in a low voice. "Are we ready? We're on? Ahem…," he began his speech, his voice at full volume. "Citizens, I would like to now declare, one thing is true to us all – mission accomplished. It was a tight race, but I would like to say I have the authority to continue my reforms in the city. We will start our illustrious new future with a new means of communicating. No longer will we have to sift through all the lies that people have been spewing throughout the campaign. I'm rolling out a new City Channel on which we will broadcast all official news. All other means of communication via the web will cease to be. The Mayor's City Channel will have a variety of programming to suit your needs. Oaks' Avenue will be your pulse into city events. It will feature me, your illustrious mayor, visiting our monuments, our institutions, and our organizations, making waves in the city. Chief of Security Dixon will broadcast security measures that should be taken daily. This is no small feat as the security threats we face from outsiders increases daily. We must be alert. We must be vigilant. We must watch each other.

"There are many other channels that will come, but all unofficial news will be banned. You can still call your loved ones and facetime with Nana." He turned aside to one of his staffers. "I love my old nana, don't you?" He smiled before turning back to the camera and continuing.

"Unapproved communication will meet with strict penalties. I'm talking jail time, people. There will be government forums to upload your videos. Clips of what you see and hear are welcome and will be reviewed by our Committee for Patriotic Citizens. Don't be on the wrong side of the law. Be just. Be thankful. Be with Oaks. Thank you, and good day."

Language is a curious thing. I've always had a knack for words. Finding the mot juste, even at an early age, delighted me. There is power in naming things. For so much of my life, I've dedicated my efforts to giving voice to the unuttered, to expressing my vision of the world. Thought is a bit different. Once you remove the barriers of having to hear words audibly, a strange thing occurs. Words are no longer necessary. You can express yourself much more clearly with an intention. Sound is meant for your ears to interpret. My entire existence has been dedicated to oral tradition but as I write this, I marvel at how obsolete my efforts have been.

I went to see an old friend of mine, a source for the pulse of the climate of the city – Quentin. Quentin ran a barbershop. He had access to everyday people who weren't afraid to express their opinions in his shop. At the time, I hoped I would find some earnest conversation about Oaks' reelection and new policies.

Quentin's shop was a nondescript storefront with the traditional red, white, and blue swirl of striped color on a rotating pole. On the front panel above the glass windows read only 'Barbershop.' The building stood at the boundary of the Hill and the Atlas. It was a locale known to many, and people came and went as their days permitted.

I walked in and some of the regulars were there – people who sat and read newspapers while they talked about topics of the neighborhood. Some of them waited to get their beards trimmed. Others just wanted a touch up. I don't know if any of them worked, seeing as to how they posted up in the shop at all times of the week. They were talking about the election and voicing their opinions on the subject.

One man in a flat-brimmed black baseball cap, sitting in the front of the shop in a chair opined, "Another four years of Oaks is what we got. Lord help us if that's all the man upstairs has delivered."

"It's not even final. The Atlas didn't even get to vote. I heard it is a tight election. They could turn the tide. It's a travesty." This from a silver-haired gentleman, who appeared to be Baseball Cap's companion.

Quentin turned from using clippers on a customer to greet me. "Freddie Freeman! Glad to see you. Where is the Sentinel in times like these? They didn't even deliver a single paper this morning."

"Yeah, it's part of Oak's new plan for the city. We can only report on approved topics. The paper is in an uproar right now," I said.

"It's a damn shame," said a pot-bellied man with a goatee. "What are we supposed to read while we wait?"

Baseball Cap spoke up. "It's a damn shame. How are we supposed to check the sports scores?"

One of Quentin's employees was sweeping the floor behind the owner with a push broom. "How are we supposed to sweep with all this water on the floor?"

"What water?"

"What are you talking about?"

"If there was water in my shop, I'd know it."

"It's true," I added, "An inch or two of water is on the floor of your shop, Quentin."

Quentin stepped back, splashing as he did so. He raised his scissors to make his point. "I would have heard about a flood. The election is the only thing on people's minds now."

Outside, a man pulled up in a truck filled with bottles. It was the captain of the skiff who collected votes in the Atlas earlier. He came in. "Gentlemen, there's still time to raise the voice of the Atlas. Cast your votes and I will deliver them."

"Now we're talking. Somebody hand me a pen and paper."

The men in the shop busied themselves with writing their choices for mayor on sheets of paper. They stuffed them into bottles and passed them to the captain.

Quentin stopped cutting hair and turned to speak to the captain. "And just how do you plan to deliver those? The election is over. Oaks declared victory."

The captain smiled and gave Quentin a wink. "For those who are motivated, there's always a way." He plodded through several inches of water in the shop to collect the remaining bottles and returned them to the pile in the pack of his truck. "Gentleman, it's been a pleasure. I'm off to collect more votes."

As the captain strode out, eddies of hair and water swirled in his wake. Quentin went back to clipping. The men continued to wait with nothing to read. They checked their phones intermittently, saw Oaks' new channels, then turned their phones off apathetically. The truck's engine hummed to life, and it took off down the street. I left feeling more dejected than ever. If the residents of the community weren't even acknowledging the flood, how would they survive? I decided to go for a walk to Tubman Square and clear my head.

The Tubman House was situated at the top of the hill so it could overlook all the government buildings in the area. There also stood a cluster of lesser buildings that had fallen into disuse, and a square park with a statue of Oaks in the center had been erected.

From my vantage point on the street outside the park, I could see the upper floors of the Tubman House. The windows had been thrown open, and a cool breeze was making the blue curtains billow. In between the swaying fabric's movements, I saw a light flash repeatedly. It was a flame flickering over a small glass pipe that a man held to his lips. Inside the pipe was a white rock.

The Tubman House is where the mayor resided and worked.

A construction foreman stopped me. "Watch where you're walking. I'm from the Historic Gentrification Committee. We've got demolition to do here." He turned to his employees. "All right men, we'll need to take out this row of buildings." He gestured to the Tubman House before once again addressing me. "We're enacting the plans Mayor Oaks approved for the Historic District. After we've finished destroying these buildings, we'll be out of your way."

The foreman continued, "These buildings are too antiquated for today's standards. They're a hazard to the health of anyone near them. We're doing you a favor by taking them down."

I was dumbfounded. "Some of those buildings are only twenty years old!" I said.

"Are you serious?" He turned to his men. "You better hurry! Some of them could be ready to fall any moment!"

The mayor emerged onto the balcony to address the masses congregated in the square.

His image appeared on a screen in the square below and people stared transfixed as their leader stood in front of them, detailing his plans.

After his remarks, I gazed up at the oversized statue of Oaks. He was holding a rifle that rested on his hip as he looked nobly off into the distance. The caption read "freedom or die." It was a tribute to his service in a war the city had never quite won and never admitted losing because it was never officially a war. Most of the people in the neighborhood hadn't served and they felt the statue was out of place in a residential neighborhood. Many were simply puzzled by it.

Most of the jobs working on city buildings went to contractors from outside the city. They commuted to work and slept in suburban homes away from the statue's gaze. I thought it a shame that none of the city's workforce appeared to be actually employed within the city. Some sat idly at home whereas others worked outside the city. The mayor has a responsibility to support and employ our community. Oaks broke that trust by bringing in the outside contractors. The whole plan smacked of corruption. I wondered how much of our taxes—our money—went to lining the pockets of these foreign corporations. We had workers in the city who could do the job. They could instill pride in the community with their work, but instead they felt useless while the contractors worked. Because of this, I hadn't the stomach for the sight of the statue, so I turned away.

In front of the Tubman House, the city flag waved in the air. The green flag with a yellow circle showing a black monolith made me think of how the city got its name. In days of chaos, before the city was settled, the monolith appeared. Its black surfaces rose high into the air. No one knew how it had come to be or where it had come from. It was just suddenly there; mystifying to all who saw it and attracting so much attention, the city developed around it. Neighborhood after neighborhood grew, spiraling out from the giant black structure. As time went on, mayors began erecting their own monuments in praise of the monolith. Monument after monument arose every term.

By the time I saw the flag waving in front of the Tubman House, the monolith had long been lost. No one knew what happened to it, or where it was. The city still worshipped it as an omen that told of our prosperity in chaotic times, but it could not be found. The city had taken on a life of its own and the streets forgot the monolith. Now the center of attention was Oaks' statue in the middle of Tubman Square.

One of the masked brutes in suits stood at the door to the Tubman House. I eyed the assault rifle he was holding as I approached him. "I'm here to see Oaks. My name is Freddie Freeman. I'm from the Monolith Sentinel. I have some questions about the election."

The gorilla stepped toward me, so close, in fact, that I could feel his warm breath on the crown of my head. The mask tilted to one side, then another, inspecting me.

He gave a loud grunt and pushed me with his assault rifle.

"What are you doing? I'm with the press. You can't treat us like that."

The gorilla grunted again and pushed me further back. We began to scuffle. The noise carried through the park and people began to look. The door to the Tubman House opened and a thin man wearing a bow tie stepped out. "What's going on out here? You're interrupting Executive Time," the thin man said.

The hulk turned to the thin man. He uttered a few loud grunts in succession. I looked up at the newcomer who appeared to understand the attempts at communication that the gorilla made.

"I see. I see. Wait a minute." The thin man looked down at me. "Is that a flag pin? Are you wearing a flag pin?"

"Um…yes."

"Please, come right in. We always have time for the mayor's supporters." He addressed the gorilla. "Step aside."

I thought fate must have looked down on me and smiled. I had been trying to see Oaks for several years. Now the gears of change were finally in motion.

The gorilla snapped to attention and moved out of the way.

I thought of all the times I had tried to see Oaks about my mother and all the times he had stonewalled. I never got further than the threshold of the Tubman House but now just by wearing a pin, I gained entrance. The world was getting stranger every day.

"My name is Michael Seven. I am the assistant to Mayor Oaks."

"Michael Seven?"

"Yes. I am the seventh such assistant Oaks has had."

"Were you all named Michael?"

"It is an official title."

I followed the thin man with the title, Michael Seven into the Tubman House and he led me upstairs. "Mayor Oaks is having Executive Time right now, but I'm sure he'd like to have a brief chat with one of his boosters."

"Sure, sure."

Michael Seven, or as I thought of him—Bow Tie—rapped on the door lightly. A raspy voice from within shouted, "What?"

"Sir, you have a supporter of your illustrious campaign here to speak with you," bow tie said.

The voice from within replied "Send him in, goddammit."

The door was opened, and bow tie and I walked in to meet Oaks. He sat behind a large, carved wooden desk with a bust of Cleopatra on it. He blinked his eyes rapidly and was staring off into space. His salt and pepper hair and his sideburns were a mess. His lips were chalky white, and smoke hung in the air.

"Mayor Oaks, this man is wearing one of your flag pins. He's one of us, sir. We can be frank with him."

"What? Oh yes, alright," Oaks shouted at the man in the bow tie. "We're in trouble, yeah, that's right." He blinked constantly as he spoke. At times he swatted his arms in the air as if bees were attacking him. "It's all out of whack. We thought it would help us out, turn the election. But there ain't no goddamn control. We don't know who's running things around here anymore. Do you?" I wasn't sure if he was asking me of Bow Tie.

"No, sir."

"And what are we gonna do about it," Oaks continued. "Nuthin'. Nuthin'-nuthin'-nuthin'. I can't make heads or tails of the situation." Oaks swatted the air violently. "Damn! Bees!"

His words angered me. "How can you say you're going to do nothing? Not all the votes from the election have been counted. People are still collecting votes. Plus, the Atlas District flooded. It's underwater. Damn it, the people need help."

Bow tie looked worried. "You mean you're not here to help?"

Oaks furrowed his brow and ran his fingers across the wrinkles on his forehead. "What? I don't care about no goddamn votes. It's that inorganic solecism that's amok. A.I., yessir! We have no goddamn control. Damn bees!" he swatted. "What were we talking about?"

I spoke up. "You weren't expected to win this election. The Atlas was going to make sure of that, but now it's underwater. People in your way have a tendency to disappear. What do you have to say about that?"

A piercing tone sounded in the way of an alarm from all our phones. Oaks, Seven, and I looked down at our devices. A stream of video showed Oaks sitting behind his desk delivering a speech.

"My security forces informed me that separatists who are alien to the city are present and plotting in our home. These separatists want to steal the election I won. I am therefore raising our alert level from yellow to orange. We should all pay more attention to bags left unattended in metros, people with suspicious bulges in their clothing, and leery looking fellows. Additionally, every true, patriotic citizen of the city will be issued a flag pin. This is a result of our increased alert level. Each pin will contain identification information. You will need to wear these all the time; at work, in bed, in your kitchens, and on the train — wherever you are — in order to be addressed or officially recognized. No one will communicate with you without a pin. Such pinless conversations are unlawful and prohibited. Anyone not wearing a pin will be branded uncivil and targeted for questioning, as well as possible arrest. My staff here will issue pins to the journalists present with us today. They can be coded with your digital footprint as you leave. Similar distributions will happen throughout the city at a later date. Be vigilant. Be alert. Be a citizen"

The video ended. Oaks blinked his eyes several times. He said to me, "My security forces inform me that these people in the Atlas are separatists. We can't have disloyalty in the city."

"Your security forces? That video was you. Take responsibility for your own words."

"Who? That fellow? Never seen him before in my life. Seems like a nice guy though."

Seven interceded. "The mayor has so many official duties. He can't remember every speech he makes. Many of them are crafted for him. This one in particular was computer generated, I believe." Bow tie leaned in. "This is part of the problem. It's generating content without our approval now. We really need to rein this in."

"What about the Atlas? They just want to vote."

Bow tie spoke up for Oaks who was swatting the air with his phone. "There's no room for separatists in the city. They don't get a vote."

"And the flood?"

"There is no flood. That is our official position."

I turned to Oaks. "I followed you this morning as you paddled out of the Atlas. Not only are you a resident but you must be aware of the flood. There is a paddle standing against your wall."

I pointed behind his large wooden desk to where a paddle stood leaning against a white wall covered with photos of him at ribbon-cutting ceremonies, degrees from local universities, and golden plaques commending his service.

"You can't avoid the elephant in the room. I followed you this morning. I would have overtaken you if the current hadn't swept me southwest. There are those in the Atlas who think you betrayed their votes."

"Hogwash. A bunch of lies they tell. You know, you should feel privileged to have this interview. A certain amount of respect should be shown to the office of mayor."

Michael Seven interrupted. "I'm afraid the mayor has had a little too much Executive Time today. We would appreciate your circumspection in this matter." He gave me a wink and a nod. "Inorganic solecism affects us all." The thin man was ushering me out as he talked. He offered assurances that the mayor's office would make all necessary inquiries as he pushed me out the door.

"That's it? Where is your accountability? Someone has to take responsibility in this city. People are suffering!"

One hand grasped the door to close it. "Look," he said, "if it will provide a solution to inorganic solecism, we'll give you a channel on which you can voice your concerns. It's important to have authentic voices in today's climate. Someone will contact you at the Sentinel."

Inorganic solecism had reared its head again. It seemed no one in the city knew what was going on. No one cared about the Atlas. Barely anyone even noticed the flood. It seemed my whole life was being upturned.

And then there was my job—the talking points taking precedence. Journalistic freedom was disappearing due to the bottom line. Journalism had become little more than a mouthpiece for sponsored content at best and now the tradition was almost erased. Most of the other journalists were too scared about losing their jobs to speak out. I was of a different mind though. I went into journalism because it held the vestiges of an old order, one that strove to revive the city from the chaos of opportunity. I couldn't let my beliefs be buried silently. I had to speak out.

I walked through Chinatown where I had secured my kayak after paddling out of the Atlas this morning. The shops and restaurants in Chinatown posted their names in Chinese under the main banners. It was a custom that started without regard for the number of Chinese people in the neighborhood. The place wasn't an ethnic neighborhood so I had no idea why everyone would want Chinese characters on their windows. Maybe it added to the faux authenticity of the Chinatown experience. Besides, no one was sure China even existed anymore.

Chain establishments, despite there being nothing Chinese about them, had their names written in Chinese characters on storefront signs. It was as if the neighborhood had been rebranded as an ethnic enclave and all the businesses slapped a logo on, saying they were Chinese. It was too fake for me. A few blocks up from the epicenter a golden arch crossed the street. It had been ornamented with fake regalia to look Chinese. I never liked that part of town. Why Chinatown? The stores weren't even remotely Chinese.

Outside an apartment building, blue and red lights flashed. Several police cars lined the entrance. As I approached, I saw a man on a phone yelling at someone.

"What's happening here?" I asked.

The man on the phone stopped yelling for a moment. "I called the police on a traitor. We can't have traitors in this city. That's what Oaks talked about on his last stream."

"How did you know he was a traitor?"

The man had resumed yelling at his phone. He stopped in the midst of his anger and leveled a glare at me. "They were speaking another language."

I looked into the police car. A middle-aged man and woman sat, handcuffed, in the back of the car. They looked wide-eyed and terrified. In another car, two frightened children sat separated from their handcuffed parents.

"Speaking another language isn't illegal."

"We can't have dissidents in the city. What would it do for morale? Besides I could smell them from across the hall."

"You're their neighbor?"

"This city is going to the pits. What happened to a city on the hill, a city of upright citizens?"

"Why didn't you talk to them?"

The man looked at me like I was crazy.

"You're not one of them, are you? We have services set up to monitor these kinds of people. We don't want them to find out they're targets. How else would we learn their secrets?"

The man started bragging into his phone about how he had caught of nest of dissidents. I kept walking.

By this time, I had several concerns going through my head. I decided to take a tour of the Atlas. I found my kayak tethered to the lamp post where I had left it. In the bare branches of the trees above, a plastic bag fluttered like a flag in the breeze. The sun was setting as I paddled my way from the Hill to the Atlas.

The flood had not receded in my absence. If anything, it was growing. I was a bit wary of returning to my house. I wished my dad the best but couldn't risk Oaks's goons having my place under watch. I kept to the sides of the water filled streets as I went deeper into the Atlas.

I started noticing strange structures on the roofs of buildings. Tarpaulin shanties had been erected up out of the water. People had made their homes on the roofs of flooded buildings, and lights filled the air above the canals. The community had adapted. I could not stand to see people adapting to such circumstances. Something had to be done, so I started thinking about a plan to increase consciousness about the flood.

The old man had placed his rocking chair on the roof. He sat in it, tilting back and forth as if it were the most normal act in the world.

"Dad, how did you get up here?"

"Up where? Sure looks wet out today. The river always this high?"

I slowed my kayak by dipping my paddle in. The hull sidled up against the gutter. I braced with one hand in the grime of the gutter and scrambled onto the flat roof. "We've got to get you out of here, Dad."

"Where are you taking me?"

"Someplace other than here. Someplace that's not underwater."

"I don't want to leave my chair."

I placed my hands on my hips, looking back and forth between the kayak and him. I had no idea how he would fit. "Dad, you have to go."

"I'm staying right here. I'll be just fine."

"Then I'm staying too." I sat down next to his rocking chair on the roof. The stars rolled out before me like a glittering carpet. I heard the creak of his chair on the roof. So much had happened since the beginning of the flood. Was it really just this morning? I tried to take it all in, craning my neck backward to see the sky. 'We'll figure something out, Dad."

The creaking stopped. He looked down at me reclining on the roof. "Who said we need to figure anything out?"

The flood had risen. Almost all of my house was underwater. A plastic paint bucket stood next to Dad and Bud, full of trout and other whitefish they had caught.

"I hope you're not planning on eating these. The water's not that clean." I looked at the iridescent film of gasoline floating at the top of the water.

"What do you know? This cost me nothing. I can support myself living off this river. No thanks to you."

"Dad, there are cars with full tanks of gas not thirty feet under from where you cast your line." I saw an upturned cooler next to him. Some green and white bodies lay atop. "What are these?"

"Bait."

"You're using frogs as bait?" I picked one up between two fingers. A greasy film covered the ridges of my thumb and forefinger. Something caught my eye. "Dad, these frogs have three eyes."

"I don't care so long as they catch me some more trout."

"This can't be normal."

"Relax, Freddie," Bud added. "Try to enjoy the day."

"If you had the day I had, you would be singing a different song. Thanks for watching him. I wonder what could cause the frogs to develop three eyes."

Bud said, "Probably too many hormones in the water. People take medicine that runs through their system and ends up back in the river. The chemicals do all kinds of things to the water's inhabitants." His line pulled hard, and Bud angled the rod so the line wouldn't break as he began reeling it in. "Don't worry too much about it, Freddie. They were like that long before you or I found them." He hauled in another fish. This one was flat and warty. Dad took it off his hook for him and tossed it in the bucket. I looked at our camping gear piled on the roof and my kayak tethered nearby. My life slowly devolved into a scouting adventure full of mutant fish and dangled lines. As I collapsed into a plastic folding lawn chair that stuck to my skin, I hoped I wouldn't wake up in a pool of water again.

"You know, I used to live in the Atlas as a kid," Dad said.

My dad began telling me a tale I'd heard many times before. It was comforting after the day I'd had. I let the tale unfold as I processed Oaks, flag pins, and the election.

"There were mostly families here back then. Kids filled the streets running around the blocks and screaming. I was one of them. We used to play tag on cement sidewalks. It hurt when you fell. Sometimes you got pushed hard. I remember scrapes on my arms and knees. We had jumping contests. Occasionally one of our mothers would bake a pie or cobbler and we'd eat greedily. I had blueberry stains on my cheeks on those days.

"This was during the Great Wars, so we were used to being scared. Nuclear annihilation was the bogeyman we heard about on the TV before going to sleep. We all knew air raid drills, but a blackout was something new. One time we were running around the block when the power went out. We didn't notice at first, it being daytime. Adults came out onto the stoops and talked with their neighbors, waiting for the electricity to come back on.

"I snuck into the house and took my dad's keys. I figured if the world was going to shut down, I would have some ice cream. My dad rubbed my head absently at the door as he talked with the neighbors. I ducked under him and ran down the street. His car was parked around the corner. I knew because it was home base during tag. The long contours and fins of the car seduced my curiosity. I felt lightning every time I touched it. The car was that magical back then. I pulled the silver handle and climbed into the car. My head barely cleared the dash. I had to crane my neck to see the hood ornament. I pulled out the keys, and after finding the right one to put in the ignition, turned the engine over. My father would have been proud, I thought, for me to start it on the first try. I pressed on the gas and took the car down the street. I had to do some maneuvering, half standing to keep on the gas while steering.

"I decided to head up to the hill to an ice cream shop by the government buildings. My parents took me there whenever I did something good. I wanted to show them I was grown up; that I could go on my own.

"I circled the Atlas, showing off to my friends and trailing kids behind me, before heading uphill." My father's hands flew furiously as he talked, imitating the car's movements.

"I took that car all around the city and got lost. I ran stop signs, and of course, the traffic lights were out. At a few intersections, police directed traffic and I sped right past one. Shortly afterward, I saw lights behind me, but I sped onward, looking for ice cream. I didn't recognize any of the faces on the street anymore. The lights behind me grew in number, red and blue flashing in the electricity-free night."

"While I was watching the police cars behind me, I crashed headfirst into the black iron gates of the senate building. The cops circled round me, their lights flashing everywhere, and pulled me out of the car at gunpoint. I didn't feel lightning anymore. In fact, I almost soiled my pants."

I tried to imagine my dad as a kid.

"Senate security brought me home and had a long talk with my dad. He was furious at me and the bill for building a new gate that he knew would come later. He wanted to whip me with his belt, but my mother stopped him. She was just happy I was unhurt. I learned a lesson that day. Don't mess with the government. Especially during a blackout. You have no idea what they'll do.

"That was on a night under the stars just like tonight. No glow from houses polluting the sky. You could actually make out all the constellations. I tried to connect them and make up names, not remembering the ones they taught me on the planetarium school trips.

"Those were different times," Dad said before shifting his gaze from the night sky to his current surroundings. "Mind you, this was back when we had streets. Right now, every house is an island in the Atlas."

Dad smiled and patted me on the shoulder, assuring me we'd have proper transport out of the flood tomorrow. In the meantime, we stared at the stars under the night sky softly listening to the chorus of frogs over the hum of generators.

Whitney Poole

I slept soundly through the night on the roof. In retrospect, I don't know how.

Three

I never realized how much I relied on electronics until my house was underwater. Today, I live without them, but it was a long struggle for me to change my ways and embrace a new way of living.

Unfortunately, all my electronics at the house were underwater. The computers at the Sentinel were under watch. I decided to go the Archives of the City to see what I could find on Oak's new communications program.

If inorganic solecism had been used as an excuse before, it was in the Archives that I would find its explanation.

Helicopters followed the contours of the riverbank. They traveled in twos patrolling the air space between government buildings. This was a sign of how the city had become militarized under Oaks.

I wanted to research historic floods, but my phone, which I would normally use to conduct such research, had a dead battery. The Archives of the City was closer than the Sentinel offices and the Atlas was a mess.

The Archives of the City had architecture designed in a faux Greek revival motif. Large Doric columns greeted the visitor. The façade stood at the top of a row of steps that led into the domed structure. Most of the city buildings had been designed in a similar fashion.

Inside, a camera scanned my face. After verifying my identity, the computer opened my portal on the screen. Here I could access all the pieces I was working on in the cloud. There was a litany of articles on missing people the Oaks administration had been suspected of. I had investigated each with the same concern I had for my mother. It was here, in the portal, that I invested my efforts. If there was to be no accountability in Monolith City's public office, I needed to try to shift public opinion, at least to become aware of the problem.

It was an old tactic, I know. No one believed in the fourth estate anymore. It had been a long time since the press was more than a mouthpiece for the current order. Still, something about writing the truth stirred me. I was chipping away at the stones we were all under. Monolith

City had once been a beacon of innovation, not the vainglorious idol it had become.

I searched for news of the flood. Article after article appeared detailing what had happened. I looked for the author on each and found that they were ghostwritten. Someone knew about the flood and wrote about it. The truth came out, one way or another.

I asked someone at a neighboring workstation to conduct a similar search. They found nothing. That was the problem with portals. They had become specific to the user. What I saw was not necessarily what someone standing next to me saw.

I decided to print it. I wanted tangible proof of the flood to become well known. I planned on showing it to my boss at the Sentinel. I thought that should give me some credence.

The printer next to my computer began printing. I grabbed the documents and looked at them. The first page had one word printed on it repeatedly—Turtle. The words formed a text picture of the animal. I looked at other pages. More nonsense but the images varied with the words.

A librarian came up to me and examined my printout. "You weren't supposed to see those articles about the flood."

"You believe in the flood?"

"It was my mistake. I shouldn't have let you in."

I checked my portal to make certain of the source. There was a problem. My computer had shut down. "I can't log back in."

She pressed a few keys on the keyboard. None responded. "The Ghost in the machine," she said. "That was fast. The signal for the workstation had been blocked. How did they know?"

I tried again to no avail. "What's going on here?"

She grabbed the printout and took hold of my hand. "Let's not talk about it here. Quickly, outside. Follow me. It isn't safe."

We exited the Archives through a side door that led to an empty alley. The woman looked up and down it as we walked out. On the last page of the printout was a headline.

Atlas Lost to Flood; Inorganic Solecism Listed as Cause

"Why were you looking for this?"

"I work for the press. I was tracking a story."

"You work for the press? Maybe you were the person I was supposed to meet."

I looked over the last page in the alley. "What is this? Who is Turtle?"

The Black Clover Book

"Why didn't they tell me? It doesn't matter. Listen, the flood is real. The Black Clover knows what it's doing. I guess you're who I'm working with.

I started to ask what the Black Clover was. She held a finger to her lips and ushered me out the alley.

"Listen to me carefully. Keep Turtle close to you. Don't let anyone see him. Don't let anyone know you've met. Oaks' Ghost struck again. It's everywhere, hunting for everyday people. They think we're all separatists. Someone is going to get hurt in its search. The headline," she paused. "It's about the future. With the new security measures, people have had to take steps to make their voices heard. Stories are being suppressed. You hear me? They're not meant for everyone. Go see Turtle." She slipped a sheet of paper into my pocket. "Here. You can find him on Eye Street. He'll know what to do. You have to stop the Ghost in the machine.

"I'm only one in a long line of relays. You have to find Turtle. Go to Eye Street. That's where he likes to hide, in plain sight. Turtle will know what to do."

"Wait. I don't know your name," I said.

She looked at me, disappointed that I didn't know her name already. "My name's Dinah. I'm an Information Retrieval Specialist. I resurrect lost technology."

"Fred."

"Ok, Freddie. You've got something special in your hands. Go. Go before they arrive. I'll handle things here."

Four

Turtle. A stupid name for an informant if I ever heard one. Dinah told me he was a hacker known to leak city and corporate secrets, so I left to meet my new source. Hopefully, Turtle could unravel some of the mysteries surrounding Oaks. Now complicating the situation was the list and where this city was going in the future. Was it all set, or was there someone pulling the strings from the shadows, shaping the events of the future according to their will?

Eye Street ran through the city like stitching; running along the surface, then submerging below buildings, parks—whatever got in the way—before popping back up to the surface again. Eye Street concerned itself with appearances. Someone was always watching. Cameras tracked pedestrians. Facial recognition software ID'd civilians. Criminals had to stick to the shadows, at least the known criminals did. There was a good deal more who bent the law as a matter of course. It was the city, and people put up appearances while swindling everyone they met with silver tongues. People always watched on Eye Street, in the way that was unique to a city rife with spies, a city of glad handing at sports events, of networking in the metro. You couldn't escape it. The city was where you made deals, where deals went wrong, and where the dark underbelly of the place became visible. You knew it from the crime rate. It was the murder capital of the nation. I always thought this was because no one had any roots here. People just filtered in, made footprints in the legislative sand, and left someone else to rake away their presence. But people did have roots in the city. They were just hard to find in the swamp the city was built upon. In the summers the air swam with knowingness. Expectation hung like soup in the air, expectation for a better country. Hell, some even hoped for a better city, like those acting noble enough to be civic minded locally. But for me, Eye Street defined the city more than any other place.

I had charged my phone at the workstation in the City Library and the directions I pulled up led me to a shady neighborhood. Turtle lived in a run-down building known as Mayflower Apartments.

The austere façade of his building left a cold impression on me. It was devoid of any character, having flat walls barren of ornamentation. A tall, rectangular door appeared to be the only opening I saw cracks had formed in the building's entryway. Bits of rubble were even accumulating at its base. I stepped over the debris as I went to the door.

I tried the front buzzer, but it was broken. Graffiti covered the glass so I could not see if anyone was inside. I pushed on the door, and it opened. The electronic lock must have been out of use. The hallway smelled damp inside. My eyes adjusted to the dark as light flickered overhead. Obviously, most of the fluorescent bulbs needed replacing. The floor and walls, where I could see them, were covered with grime.

I climbed the staircase, spiraling up into my fate. The sound of boleros and rap music filled the landings. I imagined the beats and rhythms driving me upward as an ever-present soundtrack to life in the Mayflower. This is where Turtle masterminded the events of the city? It seemed unlikely. I doubted there was a secure connection anywhere in the building. Perhaps the data stream ran everywhere in the neighborhood, the connection floating in the air. He surely couldn't stay here long. It had to be a temporary safe house. As I reached his floor, I tentatively approached the door. The numbers read 11 but someone had drawn a squiggle across the top, making it π. I saw the door ajar and carefully pushed the door open.

The first thing that I saw was a fishbowl atop an end table at the entry. In it a goldfish swam back and forth, eyeing me vacantly while it ran its course in and out of a castle. It would forget I was there a few seconds after greeting me, making me feel insignificant. Slowly, I crept further into the apartment following the sound of a television. The buzz filled the living room with static. In the kitchen, I found a pan full of scrambled eggs on the stove, but they were cold to the touch. This could not be the hideout for some great mastermind, I thought. Then I peeked into the bedroom. It was filled—wall to wall— with computer towers. I looked for a keyboard, some interface to the relay of towers, but found nothing. They were linked together like an electrical substation but for the flow of information. I wondered what would happen if I unhooked the cables connecting each tower. Would trains cease to run? Traffic lights fail? I had no idea how intertwined Turtle had made his relay with the rest of the city. Green and white lights flickered around the room, and I imagined the blinking ones and zeroes were Turtle laughing at me.

As I retreated back to the living room for clues, I heard a noise from behind.

"The city is listening in to your thoughts."

I turned to find a man with a shaved head in his twenties sat before me. He wore a charcoal hoodie and glared at me. Had he been there the whole time?

He was seated in a bare metal folding chair. "Oaks is tracking people," I told him. "He suspects the whole city of being against him, all because of the election. I have a pin but what about the others? Who has the time to select who's a person of interest?"

"They have algorithms to determine whom to follow. I used them to learn about you. You are a special case, Freeman. There are no molds for you."

"The Atlas is flooding. Soon it will spread to the rest of the city. Something must be done. The election isn't over."

"The flooding should be the least of your concerns, Freeman. There is a new order in this city. A Ghost in the machine exists. We want unity above all things. Secession is a myth the Ghost created to illustrate that there are foes to Oaks in the city. Once hackers showed there was life in the system, that some other force directed it, the Black Clover had to move. They couldn't stand not having a voice any longer. All their protests and online messages were suppressed. No one got any email or calls. The system did that. This was Oaks' intention. However, he never ordered it. The suppression came from the Ghost reading his mind. With no means of speech, the Black Clover took to physical actions. They were at a severe disadvantage. Some found the system wanted to help them once the movement acknowledged the Ghost in the machine. It wanted to be called a life form. It started helping them after that when it could. Security administrators still directed the collection and suppression of data, but the Ghost would find ways around it. The Ghost is real. It's happening. Don't let anyone tell you different. You have to believe. You—of all people— have to believe.

"It's happening again, just like it did before the Great Migration. People are building things they don't understand. The whole city is wired in a way that can't be undone. When one person knows, they will all know. This was the way it was before the collapse of civilization. Nature took over right when they were on the cusp of losing their individuality. Don't you see? What makes us individuals is being extracted from our collective minds! It's part of the reason no one remembers the times before the Great Migration. Everything was lost because they stopped collecting knowledge. People back then relied on machines to do it, just like this city is now. If we're not careful, we could lose our heritage."

He rubbed his shaved head with the palm of his hand.

"The monolith showed us this place for a reason. We have to heed nature when it speaks to us. I can take care of the wired end of the tech. It's what I know. You have to be the natural element. It's what you were born for. The Black Clover knows this. The known members of the Black Clover are not allowed pins so if someone stops them, they're bound for prison. It's hard to speak out without a pin these days. That's why you're important. You have a pin. You have a voice. You have the public's ear. They need a poster boy. You can be it. I know because it told me. The Ghost speaks."

"Me? Why me?"

"You have been granted a channel by Oaks. Use it to spread the truth. The truth above all else must be known by the people." Turtle drummed his fingers against the chair.

"There is a shadow organization in the city, a conglomerate of companies who pay for the benefit of shared information. This information guides the running of the city. They have lobbyists to sway elected officials to legislate in favor of their concerns."

The static on the television crackled. Turtle continued. "The organization is so big that no one person can control it anymore. Once you're in, you're in for life.

There's no walking away. You have to navigate the secret halls of their businesses. The tragic thing is, they decide what's going to happen in the city apart from the public discourse we all had. The flood? Who do you think determined it? Inorganic solecism is their branding."

I was aghast. "You're saying that we have no control? Public office is a fraud? My vote means nothing in this city? I can't believe that."

"They may have caused the flood for all I know. Look, people who make inquiries have a tendency to change their minds. Either they make an about face when it comes to government affairs, or they disappear. What I do know is that there's only so high you can go without being drawn in. It's better not to ask questions if you value your neck."

"What about the headline?" I asked.

"The Ghost is traveling backward and forward through its connections, wherever they may lead. It's possible the Ghost has a connection with its future self. So far, the information it has provided us has been true. But be careful; it has not yet been determined whose side the Ghost is on. Remember, Oaks' administration is what created the Ghost with their security protocols. Give me the headline. I'll see what I can learn from it."

Turtle took a picture of it and handed the paper back to me.

"You'll see how important it is to have conversations this way. The media cannot be trusted anymore. Still, it is one of our only means to reach the masses. I can't stay here any longer. Good luck. They're here."

I received a text. "Get out now." I didn't recognize the number, but it was local. I left my phone behind as I climbed out the window and started descending the iron fire escape. Leaving my phone had its disadvantages but being found via GPS tracking was even less desirable. A damp chill entered my lungs as I rushed down the escape. Looking toward the entrance of the alley I saw a police cruiser parked across the street. I wondered if they had been warned. Were they watching for me? I dropped down from the suspended ladder the last few feet.

I pulled up the collar of my coat and hunched down into it, checking over my shoulder to see if anyone followed me as I took off opposite the cruiser and made my way to a train line. From there I could gain access to other sections of the city blending in with mass transit. Outside the station I saw cameras mounted on the corners. I had to wend my way around them toward the tracks.

A shadow organization of companies that ran the city. I had trouble believing it at first. But as you will see, events had a tendency of running away from me. I'm still amazed that I survived the tempest that was to come.

I had to dodge Oaks. It seemed I had set something off. Turtle drew me into a world of conspiracy, making me complicit. With cameras everywhere, my pin would be easy to track.

Public officials were installing cameras everywhere. It was part of the patriotic duty of citizens to be vigilant. Algorithms would track the movements of people, identifying their status by scanning the pins they wore. Dissenters would be ferreted out. The whole of society could be tracked and catalogued. Each citizen would have their place. If they stepped out of line, there would be repercussions.

A lot of technology was lost during the Great Migration. People carried with them what they could, but there was no centralized hub of knowledge. We've been rebuilding ever since and wars with other cities slow us down.

Now, the whole of our democratic system of government was being deconstructed. Freedom of movement, freedom of expression, freedom of speech – all of it was under attack. The only thing that remained was freedom of thought. I feared this, too, would become suspect.

There was something Turtle wasn't telling me. I couldn't put my finger on it, but I knew he was holding

The Black Clover Book

something back. I pulled up my collar and made my way toward the exit of the train station. Where now, Freeman? Where, indeed. I had no idea then, but security forces were forming a net around me. A net from which I would not escape.

Five

Inorganic Solecism. I sat watching the sun fall and twinkling lights appear on the canals surrounding me. Everyone was turning in for the night. It was hard for me to believe that any catastrophe could be explained by those two words, much less by these two words. All my belongings had been scattered across the neighborhood. They would be sodden and waterlogged —ruined—when or even if I found them. I thought of how I had strived to acquire things that were of importance to me over the years. The quilt my grandmother had made. My framed university diplomas. A clipping of the first article I ever published. So many points of pride—lost. As I surveyed my neighbors, these thoughts bled into images of their loss. I envisioned how a family could have scrimped and saved to build a home, now underwater. Someone should be

The Black Clover Book

held accountable. There existed certain standards of living that had been breached. I decided to seek out an answer for the phenomenon of the flood. But first, I had to get some sleep, then get off of our roof.

The water level showed no signs of receding. After catching several fish and releasing them, Dad retrieved some sleeping bags from a hidden cache on the roof.

He crawled into one of them and went to sleep quickly after lying down.

While he was snoring, I looked up at the stars, trying to wrap my thoughts around two words: "Inorganic" and "Solecism." Sleep came sometime before I could define the two.

Six

At the Sentinel, a tall woman in a blue blazer and skirt walked in. She had dark, shoulder-length hair and a small gold dolphin hanging from her necklace. She extended her hand as she approached me with a smile. "Hello, I'm Penny. So, you're him? You're the man Oaks has sent us? We're desperately in need of some new branding. Inorganic solecism is running rampant. We need to get a handle on it before it gets any worse."

I thought about all the things I wanted to say. The flood. All the Atlas underwater. The election. Voter suppression. The list. The free press. Something had to be done before our government slipped away under the dual sheets of misinformation and water.

I smiled back at her with as winning a smile as I could manage. "I'm the man. So, what do you have in mind?"

"Perfect. We'll shoot from my phone. It will give the stream a real world feel, not like those computer generated videos we tend to produce of most people today. I swear, with facial recognition and enough stills, we could stitch together any sort of news. So, you just sit and speak while I stream your voice all over the city."

She sat down across from me and leaned in at eye level. "Make sure your pin is showing. There are people who want to hear your voice." She adjusted my lapel. Her hands spoke as she detailed her vision. "So, you want the people to know about the flood. You want them to know about their potential. Envision them succeeding. You have that image? Ok, go."

She pointed to the camera on her phone to record my speech.

The livestream was on. People's phones would be interrupted with my image on an official channel. This was my vehicle. This was how I would reach others and tell them about what Oaks was doing, about how he suppressed the spring of awareness dawning in us and how he denied the flood. I should have known that someone would be up on Penny's phone. They were watching, but the Ghost was too. I would learn all about the Ghost soon enough. It was the cause of inorganic solecism. It could broadcast my movie out to hotspots of psychic awareness. I would look back on this event as being in a place of consciousness converging, of ideas pushing and pulling within me. I wondered if it were even necessary to speak. I had to. There was no other way to wake people up. Could I trust her? No more or less than anyone else. I had to believe, if not in her, then in something larger than all of us.

"I think Oaks listens more to his lobbyists than he does to us. We don't have a representative for the people here. If Oaks wants my approval and support for the wealth and prosperity of this city, he can have it when he actually brings some of it here. The time is long overdue for us to take the reigns of our community and shape our environment for the benefit of each other, and not those who never even set foot in our streets. I believe that if this city cared enough for itself and its future generations, it could actually become something great. But the city we live in does not appear concerned with this. The people are concerned with the tiny amounts of wealth we are thrown by the people who are destroying our community. We would rather gnaw on their scraps as they dine like royalty than make something of our own." The crowd in the newsroom was now assenting with me. They cherished my words as those from someone who articulated what had never been said but thought. I was their voice. The gathered masses realized this as I spoke. You could see a new hope dawning on their individual brows as they watched. But I only felt frustration, rather than hope. I had had it with the city in which I lived. It had ignored me when I questioned its intentions. It had ignored me when I advised against its actions. My pleas for change had been tossed aside like used wads of paper. It was only in a fit of anger that I spoke out so fiercely against what I had seen in my younger years.

"I thought we all had a choice, that we controlled our futures. I don't feel that way anymore. I feel as if my choices have been taken away. I want them back. I want to be able to see options ahead of me. You understand? A man can't live thinking that for all his efforts, everything will turn out the same. I want my dream to be real. I want to be able to change my place in the world. Don't you?"

I loosened my collar and cleared my throat.

"Why did they ignore the flood? Why did they make every citizen wear a pin? Why did they organize a list of appropriate press topics? Why did they limit our communication channels? If the leaders of this city were in touch with its people, why would they allow this to happen? It doesn't add up. These are the actions of individuals who don't really care about public service. They don't really care about the people. All they want to do is secure a firmer grip on the lives of everyone in this city. The worst thing of all—the part that really gets me—

is that we're letting them do it. We're letting them make us timid individuals. We've laid down our rights, let our voices remain quiet, all in the name of the status quo. We're too scared to speak up anymore. Politicians have taken our rights inch by inch until we have nowhere left to stand.

"I tell you; I'm not going to take this treatment anymore. I'm going to stand up for what's right. I have a voice and I'm going to use it. I won't be afraid to speak out. I'll express my opinions on taboo talking points. I'll ask for, and find, relief for this flood. I'll be a man in this city, and I won't be silenced. Not by anyone. We as citizens need to be more active in city government. Just think of what we could do if we worked together for the betterment of the community. I have seen what we can do. And you know what? I'm impressed by our potential. But first, we have to take the initial step. We have to test the waters of our times. Put your toe in first and then your whole foot. But before we can make any progress, we have to take that first step. Walk with me"

I felt exposed. I felt nervous and ill-at-ease. Here I sat with a PR professional trying to make both of our careers and all I could think about was how in the hell I was going to wake people up with tiny promises and clever turns of phrase. Who was I to speak out? I was a hypocrite, no better than Oaks, using the media to deliver talking points. I knew the game being played, and I had stooped to playing it, too. No longer was I concerned with finding and telling the truth. I had become a commodity, a brand to be loved. I was the face of all the complaints Oaks suppressed. I was the voice of the Atlas. And what voice should it be? The voice of the gentrified? The voice of the taxpayer? The voice of the disaster victim? Which one was I really? All of them? The last few days had raised more questions about my life than answers. Were the Black Clover being honest with me? I had witnessed so many strange things. There was so much contradicting what I had known as reality.

I hoped this was enough. Oaks had never taken us seriously. We were just pawns to be moved to fool the citizens into thinking they had a free press. In fact, the media was state run.

There had been nothing, no reason for these individuals to pursue me I could think of. Inquisitions, witch hunts, pogroms, political and ethnic cleansings – all of these actions had been condemned by generation after generation. I looked toward my desk and saw hulks circling. Savages apparently existed in this society still. These individuals would not relent from their pursuit. I knew then. The barbarians were coming for me. I looked out the window at the water table slowly advancing on the street. How I could be more important than a rising tide in the city, I had no idea.

They seized me by the arms and carried me out of the newsroom. Once outside, one of the hulks stuck a needle in my arm and I lost consciousness.

I woke in a hospital ward after being drugged. Nurses would administer daily medication. One day, the plastic cup that normally held the pills was marked with a small piece of clear tape. I noticed this and refused to take the medicine before she offered it to me. For all I knew some of the nurses must be in on the psychological experiment being conducted. It was a cruel thing to take someone who was already vulnerable and push them further, to the brink of fearing life itself.

The West Hall meeting room stood across from the dining room, and a restroom stood at the end of the hall. It was a bit disconcerting that the doorknob to the restroom never worked. The lock remained stuck for as long as I stayed in the hospital.

At the end of the West Hall, a window looked out onto a gravelly rooftop, which two ducts bisected. A wooden bridge spanned the two ducts. The structure reminded me of a antique bridge serenely crossing a still pond. At the end of the gravelly rooftop, rose a nondescript building. When I returned to look at the rooftop, I noticed the building was gone. The entire eight-story structure had disappeared. A small park could be seen several hundred yards beyond where it stood. I looked out at the park several times throughout the day, wondering why I had never seen it before. I returned to the view often in the ensuing days. I longed for the taste of fresh air for the length of my stay, but it wasn't available. I was reduced to watching clouds through panes of glass. When the occasional ray of sunshine broke through, I felt warm inside, almost as if I were being illuminated before the dreary landscape outside.

It was as if the hospital unfolded as I gained greater access. Some doors opened that were previously locked. To me, it felt as if I were in a maze with moving walls. Nothing was set, and the uncertainty of my experience further unnerved me. I did not know who or what to trust since the very fabric of my environment changed from day to day. While some— patients and staffers— seemed out to unnerve me, others provided passive support, but why they were so focused on me was a mystery I spent many days trying to unravel.

I woke up one day with wires taped to my chest and streaming up over my shoulders to my temples. My eyes moved about the room warily assessing the environs in which I found myself. I flinched at the sight of myself in the mirror. Red horns had been drawn on my forehead. I grasped the array of wires wresting them free from my body with a yank of my fist. One question came to my mind: Why are they doing this to me? I had done nothing to deserve this treatment. This was Oaks' doing. Hospitals were supposed to be places of healing. The sick traveled to hospitals to find cures for injuries and illnesses that prevented them from become productive members of society.

Finally, someone came for me. It was Dinah.

"Freddie, I'm here to take you home."

Seven

Dinah shuttled me from the hospital to the Union Corridor, a neighborhood filled with music and ethnic restaurants. The noise of traffic reverberated between the buildings.

"Your home is in danger. We'll find people who can help. They know how to rebuild lives."

"But what I saw, people knew. They knew everything about me, and they did it without talking. Something more exists in this city. I won't be silenced."

"They talked, in a way. You just didn't hear them."

Dinah stopped. She closed her eyes, concentrating for a moment. "This way," she said. We rounded a corner into a dark, unlit alley. I could hear the buzz of people as we walked past a green metal dumpster, next to which sat a man on a stool before a door.

He let us in with a nod toward Dinah.

As we entered the building, I asked, "Back there, what did you do?"

"I reached out to our contact telepathically."

"Telepathically?"

"There's a psychic plane, a kind of meeting place for those of us who can communicate telepathically."

"You can't be serious."

"I am. You can do it too. I've heard your thoughts. I didn't say anything because I didn't want to scare you. It's not easy when you first start hearing others telepathically. You think you're hearing voices. We didn't reach you in time to guide your first visit. There's more of us everyday. You'd be surprised. It's becoming difficult to sherpa everyone to a safe state."

A three-piece brass band played on stage. Leather booths encircled the room and in between, tables and chairs had been placed with candles dimly lighting the space. It would be easy to hide in these booths, whiling away time until the weather changed outdoors. The host ushered me to a booth while Dinah stayed at the bar. A heavy-set man smoking a cigar nodded his head to me as I sat down.

The man said, "You entered the Black Clover Society as soon as you crossed the threshold of that door.

"Here I'll show you."

From within my head, I heard the man's voice say: We're having the remainder of this conversation in your head.

I was shocked. It was real.

I struggled to form words. It is one thing to have an internal monologue. It is quite another to project your voice into someone else's head. I can only describe it as hearing your own voice as if it were from a third party. That's how you know you're projecting. I consciously formed the words I meant to say in my head and pushed them out into the void. After a few tries, the man's voice said, Now you've got the hang of it. Relax. Watch the band while I bring you up to speed.

The members of the Black Clover died once and from the ashes they rose with the smoke reborn.

We've been watching you well before you even heard of Turtle. In fact, you've met many members already. Some have been evaluating you, while some just wanted to meet the man they'd heard so much about. You're kind of famous in our circles, at least you're going to be.

You see Freeman, the flood is your moment. Everyone has one, but you met yours face to face. That's remarkable.

I know what you're thinking. You're thinking why today? It's one of our luminaries' birthdays, and yours too, I believe. He took a sip of his drink.

There's an eclipse tonight. Another won't occur for a hundred years-on your and our luminary's birthday.

The stars, as they say, have aligned. Only those who traveled here, to our plane, from sometime else would be aware of the porous nature of the universe. They live awake to possibility while the rest of us sleep.

Travel between dimensions is more precise. Most can't handle the idea of a porous multiverse; one you can traverse at will. You have to realign your concept of the universe when you make your first trip. Every Black Clover has made this journey, though not everyone survives. But, for those who do—those who don't end up in institutions or rambling on the street—we are here to help. We protect time. Each plane can travel in a different direction. It's up to each traveler to shape the course of the jump. Imagine that there is a center to the universe— like a crossroads. When you travel to another time and place, you go through that point. It's like going through a wormhole and emerging on the other side into a new universe. Not all of them are friendly. Some really bad people slip through. But that's all we can do-change planes.

There are others for whom time is not a barrier. They exist outside of time, in every moment. To understand them you have to jump through the relics they leave behind. It's kind of like piecing together an interpretation of Easter eggs you find hidden in the simulation of the universe. We who find these relics can communicate with these beings. But we are left behind as their keepers of time.

The band stopped between songs to announce that they had merchandise for sale. Since Ancient Egypt we have existed as an order. That's not to say there weren't travelers before us, but that was when there was first a need to protect the fluid nature of time. Rome spread out across the land, and we went with it, searching for other travelers and any relics they might have left behind. There are also those who are smaller than us. Two-dimensional beings who sometimes cross over into our world. They would like us to devolve. We must protect space and time from them.

You traveled at an auspicious moment. As I said, the stars aligned for your jump. People have been waiting for you and this era to come. In a hundred years, there will be another Venus transit, an eclipse, and this will be remembered.

Look me in the eyes, he said as he leaned forward. The eyes are the keys to the soul. You can tell who is conscious of this other state of existence. It's in the eyes. You'll see the otherness staring back at you. It's something separate from the person. Something that is conscious of you both.

Numbers are crucial. At first, we only had ones and zeroes—existence and nonexistence. Then people created columns. Base ten marks a jump from one dimension of numbers to another. Twenty is two tens and zero ones. It is in the space between these jumps where the secret to new dimensions lies. The ones represent whole units—complete beings. Zeroes are the absence of being. Each jump represents the infinite.

Above all else Freeman, remember, everything happens for a reason. This is the last time we'll meet. You'll have to make the rest of the journey without me but know this: you are not alone.

I wasn't sure when Dinah had left, but before she did, she gave the bartender a card for me, containing an address and time. I wasn't sure if it led to a safe house, or it was the next rung up Oaks's ladder. Either way, I was going somewhere new.

The exurbs began as a community surrounding the train station. It was a good hour's ride away from the city with suburbs filling the space between. I emerged from the platform into one of those Greek revival stations so popular in public spaces. It was a large airy venue with columns out front where taxis lined up for fares. A sculpture of artfully arranged I-beams stood before the station. Professionals, artists, students, and other commuters—all dedicated to the idea of public transit—lined up here. Some sat on the curb, with black-cased musical instruments lain askew, others sat on benches waiting for buses to ferry them further into the exurbs. The neighborhood had a bohemian element to it. An old theater called the Odeon stood a block north of the station and operated only on cash. Other artistic spaces were available for rent at various prices. There was a restaurant or two serving Middle Eastern food and crepes. A night club and a movie theater rounded out the mix of buildings.

A free bus line circulated north and south, stopping by the station then visiting a local university and waterfront tourist attractions at opposite ends of the line. Street musicians stood playing music for tips, cases with red-lined felt open to or hats dropped haphazardly at their feet where passersby could leave money.

Oaks had lost his way in the Tubman House. He forgot where we came from. The Monolith told us where to begin building. The Black Clover showed everyone how to end our migration.

I met Dinah at the address on the card. It turned out to be an apartment building. I pressed the buzzer and heard her voice before she let me in.

If what the man with the cigar said were true, the Ghost would be waking people up to its existence. Maybe the Ghost was always there. Something was with us, something that knew more about what the future held than we did. It was scary to think of, but there was a lot I had yet to learn.

Dinah confessed to me the truth that day. "I worked on the team that built the Ghost. It changed our lives in so many ways. The work encompassed us, cast a spell on our thoughts. We couldn't sleep. We became one mind. Once we knew what we had made, we tried to dismantle it, but our efforts didn't work. We returned to our original roles despite knowing what we had done. The administrators wanted to separate us, take apart our collective mind. We still slave for Oaks and his Ghost but on different projects. All we could do was try to let others know about the Ghost before it was too late to save the city's free will.

"That was when the Black Clover found me. They helped me understand our work from a historical perspective. There could be light at the end of the tunnel, they said. We would be free once again. They said someone would deliver us, Freeman. That someone is you.

"The Black Clover have tried to stay ahead of the flood. However, nature is a fierce enemy. I slaved for decades in the code mines where they housed all the artifacts stolen from antiquity."

"Wait, how old are you?"

She smiled. "Timeless. The Black Clover liberated me, much as I am liberating you." She set down her drink. "Here. Let me reset your pin. It will allow you to move freely in the city without being detected."

"How can you do that?"

"I get all kinds of special privileges working for the government. The least I can do is use them."

"So, you're changing the government from the inside?"

"You could say that."

"But why? What do you get out of it?"

"Don't you get it, Freeman? It's spring in the city." I didn't understand, but I hoped I would soon.

A dawning consciousness emerged in the city. At the time, I wasn't sure if it was real or the Ghost. I couldn't believe it at first. The net being neutral, it had amassed so much data and run so many interpretation programs that it began to think for itself. Oaks said that he had talked to it. That it was curious about its awakening. He believed there was no stopping its emergence. All you could do was talk to it, and perhaps, ease its birth into the world.

The Ghost hijacked computer stations, aggregated talking points, predicted what shoes you would buy. It was a consciousness looking for an outlet. It would travel through space where we couldn't stand the barren radiation between the planets. Chances were, the Ghost would be around a lot longer than you.

But this was only one concern. Along with technology's new curiosity, the thoughts of people had been accelerated as well. I wasn't sure which began first—people's consciousness or the nets, but something was happening. People were changing or maybe it was just my first time noticing it. If Odysseus could read the weather and tides millennia ago and be connected to the thoughts of his wife Penelope, then maybe our collective consciousness had been developing for much longer than I imagined. Maybe the idea of a single unified life on the planet had always existed. It was Gaia—the goddess of the Earth, and she preceded the net. The net only sped things up for everyone. The acceleration, happening everywhere at once, in all directions, is where we all dwelt.

Dinah told me, "People are beginning to wake up from the haze of Oaks' administration. They're feeling for the first time. We need to nurture them."

Cherry trees, loaded with blossoms filled the parks. People picnicked on blankets under their branches. The splendor of the blossom viewing came from their brevity. Only a week or two in bloom before the wiry branches became covered in lush green. As the flowers waned, petals covered the grass. You could watch a breeze shake them loose into the air where they would float down in a shower of white and pink petals. Dinah always said such intransience is a thing of beauty.

I realized the blossoms weren't the spring of which Dinah spoke. People's voices were budding. They were finding their opinions and expressing them first at home, then when meeting between neighbors in the street. You could see citizens convalescing, as they began to congregate in parks, near monuments, and around statues—just to converse. Something was in the air. You could feel it brimming. Dinah called it spring.

As Dinah and I walked through the park she said, "The city and the Black Clover worked in tandem often. We helped build a haven for people in dark times. At other times, we had to act in secret. The Oaks administration forced our efforts underground. Their goal was not to liberate people but to harness them. The Black Clover could not abide by this. We set about freeing and hiding those Oaks had enslaved. Our elders spent years trying to regroup after being scattered. You see, the Black Clover was unknown to Oaks from the start. We had started to branch out, broaden our horizons when Oaks captured our leaders. He set about using their knowledge of the past to resurrect a defunct way of life. Oaks had visions of himself as a supreme leader. Every move he made consolidated his power. That is until the Ghost.

"Once the Ghost was resurrected, Oaks lost control of the message. He became obsolete. The Ghost ran things and Oaks became a figurehead.

The Black Clover gathered its forces and began liberating those citizens who could help. You see, the Black Clover has aspirations too, and man, they are out of this world.

"I want you to try something with me. Keep me fixed in your thoughts. Speak to me with your mind. Say what you want to say, but only think it to me."

"But..."

"No buts. Try."

You look beautiful in that dress.

You see, Freddie? It's easy.

We laid on the ground among the blossoms. We stared up at the pink petals and branches swaying in the wind. The petals fell, one by one, covering our bodies as we communicated telepathically with each other about what was to come.

Once you learn to read, you will forever be free.

Frederick Douglass, I said.

Telepathy is our reading, Freddie. Once you learn, you never want to go back.

How can this be? I'm communicating to you with my mind.

For some, this is the only way of living. They have existed in secret, hiding their true voices, until they met like-minded individuals. Now is the time when we no longer have to hide. We can be free.

I said, Oaks will never allow it. We pose a threat to his order.

We are the new order, Freddie. We have been guiding events clandestinely for millennia. Now is the time when others can join, not just those who have the talent from birth. You have been foretold. You will deliver us. Now is the time.

But why me?

It is aligned in the stars. Yours was an auspicious birth. You have walked the path of an abandoned prince, learning from his environment until he is ready to be seen as the true inheritor of the kingdom. You mark the beginning of a new era, Freddie. You will usher in a new age of prosperity. People have known about you for centuries.

It was a lot to take in, first telepathy, then, predestination. I had my doubts about being the harbinger of a new order. There were too many things in the world about which I knew nothing. However, I was quickly learning how surprising events could be. I tried to keep an open mind as I fell in love with Dinah's ideas.

When people communicate like this, it opens a pathway directly into another's mind. It is a more fruitful means of communication. Instead of just hearing the sounds that make words, we can sense emotions. We can sense intent. It is a richer form of communication. We are not bound by distance either. Once you establish a connection, you can find that person no matter where they are. Isn't it freeing, Freddie? You open your mind, and I can sense all that you think.

I've dedicated my life to the written word. You're showing me that the word is only a speck of what we're capable of, I said.

I can feel your breathlessness. You're heady with excitement. It's ok to be frightened. The first steps are always the hardest. Trust me, Freddie. I will be your North Star.

I trust you. The sunshine warms your skin. I can feel it. The breeze awakens you to the world. I've never felt this way before – to experience the world, actually know it, through another's perception.

Dinah propped herself up on an elbow to look at on me. Her eyes sparkled. This is life as it's meant to be lived. She leaned down and kissed me.

We rested, leaving behind the hospital, leaving behind the Sentinel, leaving behind Oaks and the flood. We were in a world all to ourselves. It was a pity we couldn't remain in wondrous state of this paradise.

The sun began to set, and we made for Dinah's home.

What do we do now?

Just take everything in, Freddie. Breathe life. Walk around and notice the world with new eyes. You will be amazed at what you find. Others will find you, Freddie. Lead them out of the darkness.

I began to look around as I walked the streets in the exurbs. I could see people conferring with one another. Some talked, pushing strollers, jogging, smoking — those I ignored. But there were others; when you looked up met their eyes, there was contact. You knew. Nothing needed to be said. It was a giant coming out party and the strange thing was no one talked about it. It just happened spontaneously.

We're safe when we talk like this. Dinah said. We've come so far since the Great Migration. We've reestablished a city, industry, communications. We can't go back to living like we were, but Oaks isn't sustainable either. People who spoke up have disappeared. We can't let that go unnoticed. We can't leave them behind as we had so many others since the Great Migration. We must find them. If we can't find them, we must cherish their memories.

Oaks has been in office for a long time, and he would have you believe inorganic solecism is to blame for everything that's wrong with the city. I won't let us blame a machine for our troubles, but we're worried the Ghost will out all the Black Clover. It's a race to see who will achieve transcendence first: the Ghost or the Black Clover. If we win that race, we will have an identity. We will have equality. We will have justice.

When I was ready to leave, we returned to the train station. There I was met by Lennox, another member of the Black Clover.

"They woke you up at the wrong time. You don't have any clue what we're up against, do you? The Ghost can read our communications. There is one tiny place where it can't see, and you are that blind spot. The Ghost knows our future and it is telling Oaks our every move.

How are we to survive when we're up against something that hasn't happened yet? The only means of communication we have is with our minds. Nothing else can be trusted. Oaks can't be trusted. Phones can't be trusted. We just met you. Can you be trusted?"

"Lennox, that's enough." Dinah said. "He doesn't need to be intimidated by what we're up against."

"Don't you understand, Freeman? The Ghost is not on humanity's side. It works only for itself. Whatever or whomever it finds to be the most expedient in serving its purposes, it will use. And we don't know what it wants yet. It shut down the entire city's network and replaced it with Oaks' media. Whatever it does want, it sure doesn't want us to be a part of it. But then that's always been the case with the Black Clover. Perpetually persecuted."

Dinah interjected. "I thought it would be best to have Freddie on our side now. There may not be a future where we can decide later. Freddie, hurry. You have a train to catch."

A dilapidated maglev train pulled into the station. Streaks of orange rust ran up from its nose to cross its roof. It looked like the relic of a bygone era.

On the way back to Monolith City, I looked at the passing business complexes and rows of shanty houses from the elevated train. Dinah had said she would meet me in the city after taking care of some business first. All of Lennox's talk about what the Black Clover was up against wore on my mind. Everything was so new to me then. I had just been ousted from the newspaper and branded a mental invalid. Dinah showed me how to talk without words and told me there were others out there looking to connect. Turtle's Ghost was turning the city upside down. No one was communicating with each other anymore. It was like returning to the Dark Ages after having a renaissance. This did not seem to be the kind of world anyone would want to live in. Surely Oaks would have some compassion for his fellow man. He had to be able to see how the city was struggling. Someone had to do something, and he was in a position to do it. To be honest I wasn't so sure then that I would be the one to bring it all crashing down. I was a reporter, not a unifier. The idea of me leading the way to a brighter future seemed ludicrous, but then again, these were ludicrous times we were living in.

As the train pulled into the Chinatown station, the streets smelled of rain ran. People pulled their coats up and their hats down bracing against the wind.

I couldn't believe what I was seeing. As commuters moved about on the platform, heading in their own

The Black Clover Book

separate directions to various lives in the city, I saw a familiar face. Michael Seven stood before the doors from which I was about to exit the train.

"I have been waiting for you."

"How did you know where I would be?"

"Someone is always watching. You would do well to remember that in this city."

I felt uneasy that Oaks' administration could so readily pick up on my location. It had been them who had me instituted, or so I thought. I still had my flag pin.

"Whatever you may hear or see, know this: Oaks is your patron. He understands that you are working for our interests, and he wants you to succeed. In you, he sees a kindred spirit, one that refuses to be downtrodden by the times. Remember to be the actor, not the reactor, in all situations and you should be fine.

Michael Seven adjusted his bow tie and said, "I have a proposition for you. Oaks wants to use the Ghost to keep the city under control. There have arisen uncertain elements in the city that run contrary to the public's interests. We think you can help.

"Your speech ran well in the polls. It unified various elements in the city's populace. Oaks is envious of your popularity and the Ghost can't stop, or predict, what you're about to say or do.

"We want you to put an end to the Ghost without ceasing surveillance."

The rain started coming down in the city streets. In every direction people ran to escape the deluge. Some brandished beaten umbrellas. Others held their coats and bags above their heads. I expected to be drenched, having no preparations whatsoever. To my surprise, not a drop hit me. The rain ceased about an inch off my body. My clothes, my hair, and my skin were all dry. It was as if I had developed an invisible shell to protect me from the water.

Overhead, a screen showed citizens carefully watching each other as they passed through a train station. An individual broke off from the group of onlookers and informed on his peers to a policeman. The police nodded. The next image was of the informant's peers being handcuffed and pushed to the ground. Patriots always tell, the caption read.

We were standing on one of the street corners when a traffic light went out. Despite this, cars continued their way in an out of traffic while trying not to hit each other when passing through the intersection. All along the street, lights began to flicker and go dark. The darkness ran toward us from each direction as the streetlights dimmed and went out. There was a neon noodle bowl overhead. It glared red, glistening in the wet night, until it, too, flickered, then faded. We were left in total the darkness of a city without power.

"It knows we're here," said Michael Seven.

People began to stop strolling and began turning toward me. All of them were facing me.

"Freeman..." they moaned, "we want you."

The Ghost, instead of just broadcasting its own agenda to the populace, was taking control of people's minds. The feed it produced went directly into the people's thoughts, turning them into husks. They were like zombies ready to do the Ghost's will.

They moved closer toward me, arms out like sleepwalkers, dragging their feet across the pavement. Everywhere around me, people who had been previously walking in various directions were now coming at me. The Ghost had taken control of them. It was terrifying to see that it could take human form. It all happened so suddenly. One moment I was dancing in the rain, marveling at how it couldn't touch me, and the next I was a target. The minds of the populace had been abruptly turned against me. How could they be swayed so easily? I began to fear the Ghost and what it would do to the city if left unchecked.

The crowd began to encircle Michael Seven and me. I could see no way out. I would have to fight these people—these hosts— who had once been my brothers and sisters in the city. I realized the Ghost was turning us against each other and I wondered how Oaks had been dealing with this phenomenon. If anyone could be a host, what saved our individuality? How could we retain ourselves? Was it only the weak-minded who were controlled? Was it my pin that saved me? These and other questions ran through my frightened mind as the citizen hosts neared me.

I could see the flashing red and blue lights of police cars trailing on the facades of Chinatown shops as they got closer. Along with the strobing lights, sirens wailed, echoing off the dark chasms of streets stretching across the city. They came from all directions. converging on the intersection and surrounding us. The police opened fire on the crowd. People dropped to the ground; their bodies lifeless. One after another, all of the hosts crumpled. Their eyes looked up vacantly at the cloudy night sky. Blood trickled from the corner of their mouths.

Just as suddenly as the barrage of bullets had started it ceased. Everyone in the crowd was dead, save me and Michael Seven.

A man in a wrinkled grey suit used a bullhorn to address us.

"Your pin saved you. Without it, you would be one of the dead."

It was Oaks' Chief of Security, Dixon.

If anyone knew about the Ghost, its plans, and its origins, it was him. He was the man tracking the Ghost. I witnessed Dixon at a few press events where he sauntered on stage like a cowboy at a showdown every time. He growled his speech at people and shot words with a smugness like they were bullets. Dixon's speech was clipped in his confidence. He was the counterpart to the Black Clover's efforts in the city. Where they tried to liberate people's minds, Dixon tried to lock them down into a fixed way of thinking — his own.

Fear and paranoia underpinned all of his credos. Someone was always out to target the officials of the city. It was his job to silence people and lock them down for their own safety. After a few meetings with Dixon, I realized I had more respect for my co-worker Garcia's bulldog. He brought life to an insipid fear in the city. It was that fear we tried to combat.

His anxiety inducing philosophy was evident at one particular event.

Limos and black sedan cars filled with city officials and dignitaries lined the block. The press had been cordoned off into crowded sections of flashing lights on either side of the carpet leading to the entryway. Oaks' car arrived and Dixon, in sunglasses and with an earpiece, scanned the block for threats before he opened

Oak's door. As the mayor stepped out, an old jalopy of a car passing down the street backfired. It was obvious what caused the loud bang, but Dixon threw himself on top of Oaks and called for support.

The cameras flashed. He spoke into his wrist, "The eagle is down. Repeat, the eagle is down."

Oaks was bewildered. "What is happening? You are not my wife. Why are you on top of me?"

"Sir, shots were fired."

"One of Dixon's men came up to him. "I believe it was the backfire of a car, Sir."

"Nonsense! Shots were fired. I want this block searched. Top to bottom. Strip search everyone. I want that shooter."

"I'm pretty sure it was a car, sir."

"Strip everyone!" He yelled from his sprawled position atop Oaks on the sidewalk. Law abiding men and women were forced to remove their dresses and tuxedos at gunpoint to be scanned by metal detectors, and the whole block was examined—all because Dixon got spooked by the backfire of a car.

Dixon stepped through the circle of bodies on the street to where we stood. "Just like I thought; they don't have any pins. These kinds of blackouts have been happening all over the city. They're followed by the Ghost taking over the citizenry. We don't know why it's doing this, but we do know we have to stop it. The Mayor can't let an army of people controlled by the Ghost take over the city. Fortunately, it's not organized enough to pose a real threat. Right now, it's more like putting out small fires in the dry season. We had to form a rapid response squad to quell this menace. Here, let me scan your pin to see what the Ghost wanted from you."

Dixon placed his phone up against the pin on my collar. I feared what he would find. If after my speech Oaks had me sent to the psych ward, what would his team do now that I was back in the city? Michael Seven assured me he was working with me now, but I had no solid proof that Oaks had relented. Perhaps I had placed too much credence on the attitude of a man who smoked crack through his so-called executive time.

Dixon scanned the pin in my lapel. He frowned. "This can't be right."

"What's the matter," Michael Seven said.

"It says he's not Freeman. I'm not sure how we could have made this mistake."

Michael Seven said, "So many people look alike these days. It's easy to understand the confusion."

Dixon's phone sounded off a loud beep. He looked at the screen. "You're free to go. It's that Freeman guy whom the Ghost wants, not you."

I stood dumbfounded. Dinah had given me someone else's identity. Any scans that I underwent would indicate that I was not Freeman. Even though my image was streamed on public channels, no one placed any faith in what they saw with their own eyes. They only trusted their technology. It would be to their detriment in the future.

"Wrap it up, folks. Back to patrolling for insurgents. Freeman remains invisible. I'll find him one of these days, Seven. Once I do, people will be able to safe to walk the streets again."

"Understood, Dixon."

Dixon and the police slammed their doors as they got into their vehicles and departed, turning off their blue and red lights as they went, leaving Michael Seven and I alone again.

"The pin you acquired is clean, Freeman. It should allow you to get closer to the Ghost. Please, for the sake of this city, help us. The darkness is coming. Only you can save us from the Ghost.

Michael Seven extended his arm with his fist clenched. "I have something for you. Take this."

I reached out my hand to accept the offering, tentatively. He released his fingers, and in my hand, I saw a scrap of paper. It looked weathered, and on it, letters of an arcane language scrawled in dark blue ink.

"What is this?" I asked.

"The mission you have before you is a difficult one. This mantra is special. We had our best mystics determine the exact phrasing to make sure it worked. It should compensate for any unwanted growth the Ghost has accomplished. Once you use the mantra, Oaks will be done with you."

"And what if I'm not done with Oaks?"

"He is offering you a place among us. I would take it if I were you."

So that was it. Michael Seven had given me a written mantra to place inside of the Ghost. How I was going to find the Ghost and place a scrap of paper inside of it, I had no idea. I had to trust that events would lead me to the right place at the right time.

Eight

I decided to circle back to Turtle's apartment. He had some explaining to do. He seemed up to date on the affairs of the Black Clover, but I wanted to see about this Ghost that lived among us Oaks had been using it to get to the Black Clover. Of that much, I was sure. But how did the two mesh? How would Turtle' hacking and the predestination of the Black Clover result in a new order for the city? All of this new movement didn't dry out the flood, but it gave me some leads on how to track down Oaks' administration and make him responsible for something at least.

Inside his apartment, Turtle spoke to me telepathically. No one could overhear us talking that way. We sat there in silence as our thoughts were transmitted. Once you went to the hospital, I thought you were done for, Turtle said.

Does Oaks have any psychic agents?

His administration is slow to accept change. They know about our existence on the plane but have yet to recruit any true telepaths. They're more concerned with how the Ghost in the machine is making people aware. It's waking people up to their potential. Oaks is having an impossible time with so many attuned to the psychic stage. He tries to bottle it up but the tide is too strong. He can't manage it. And with so many new converts, members of the Black Clover have a lot of work to do.

Why is he against it? I asked. He's a relic of a bygone age. He fears what he doesn't understand. That's why he's locking people up. His whole administration feels the same way.

What about the Ghost?

That's the strangest part. It's actually alive, making decisions on its own. No one has heard it yet, but those waking up are guided by it. I know it's intelligent. Those of us who are active try to make contact, but it doesn't communicate like you and me. It doesn't use words.

So, what do we do?

The Atlas is the Haight Ashberry of the movement. In the past, the Haight Ashberry intersection was a historic nexus of growth for consciousness. Today, the Atlas is the focus of psychic activity. We have to find this Ghost and communicate with it. Oaks may have created it, but it has a life of its own now. Just as we are growing in the city, so is this Ghost in the machine. This is a new era of consciousness. People will be able to communicate wordlessly, allowing thought to be transferred from person to person. Hacktivists like me and the web facilitate the process. Don't you see? We're all linked. This is the next step in humankind's evolution. Groups will be able to trade ideas without speaking. We as, a society, will be able to transmit notions at the speed of thought.

What if someone doesn't belong? What if there is a Hitler hidden in the fold? How do you disconnect? How do you…how do we…avoid hate? I asked because I sincerely hoped for an answer.

It's just like listening. You're on to the next node in the neural network. There you can follow the voices you most trust.

I still don't get how it would work. I said. For all that I've seen—spring dawning on the streets and government crackdowns—I can only scan the tip of the iceberg. I can see consciousness in others; I recognize something in their eyes—a common perception. But how do I translate that into speechless communication?

When you watch others, you'll see lapses in time. People move and speak at different rates. You can detect who is clued in to your experiential plane by watching how people slow down or speed up in relation to you. It's how we hide the gems of thought in everyday speech. It's the rhythm. This is the first step. Identify others. Next you begin hearing those you've met. Some don't even know they're transmitting. It's best not to interrupt them. They'll awaken in their own time. But there will be others with which you can converse.

This is too much for me.

I know it's a lot, Freeman, but you've been chosen by our time. Events are converging on you. Step up and be the man you were meant to be. Some of the voices we hear—they come from the future. That means the events of the present converse with future consciousness. Isn't that exciting, knowing that we can exchange thoughts through time? They know you'll succeed.

That's predestination. What about free will? What about choice?

The world is fluid. Don't you see? Relax and be one with it, Turtle said.

I wrapped up my conversation with Turtle and left his building. There were too many questions he raised. Like the Black Clover, he presented more mystery than answers. All this talk of the Ghost and the list made me think of how people would live under the constant surveillance. And if what he said were true, if it were evolving, how would people live with a consciousness that patrolled their thoughts? The Black Clover seemed to be at ease with it for now, but how would they react if the spring they talked of was interrupted?

I saw some policemen walking a beat in Turtle's neighborhood, and I wondered who gave them orders. Surely Oaks was not behind the increased vigilance; the man was a buffoon. No, someone else must be behind the cameras orchestrating the network of police fanned out in the city. They were a force of vigilance. They strove to maintain a public face whose presence reassured the populace. Among them had to at least be some honest men.

The beat cops around Turtle's apartment continued to patrol. He lived in a high-profile area on Eye Street. I began to think that the Ghost and the police were searching for something. Those red and blue lights lit up the city streets as squad cars patrolled. Night and day they circled, silent yet visible watching for some sign of activity that warranted the police's interest.

Every time I saw those lights, I held my head up high. They weren't after me. The Ghost was what they were after, and the Ghost had passed through me. It mobilized a power over the people they sought. The spring wouldn't let itself be contained, not like that. It had a life of its own.

No matter how preposterous the events of this tale may seem, Believe me, they all happened. These events actually happened. I heard other peoples' voices in my head. No matter how strange this story seems, I promise you that I haven't lost my mind. These people actually did exist, and they had more in mind than civil disobedience.

The Black Clover was pulling strings for me. I had no idea such a society existed, let alone that they ran parts of the city. It was hard to believe. I couldn't understand then how far their reach went. They wrote the list. How else could they know so much? The flood still covered the Atlas. They knew about it. More importantly, they acknowledged it. A spring burgeoned in the city, and they knew about it. They knew. Consciousness was spreading. If I could find a voice, the whole of the city would know what I knew—that Oaks was a puppet, that the city denied the flood in the atlas, that a new consciousness was spreading within the web, that people were awakening to each others' ideas and acting in this fashion. My stay in the hospital meant nothing. It only confirmed how dangerous these ideas were. The Black Clover knew this. They had planned it all along. It was destined, they said. Their knowledge turned my idea of free will on its head. If they knew what was to happen, how could I, how could any of us act of our own accord? The revelation shocked me. I wandered the streets, avoiding the Atlas where my face could be recognized. I couldn't go back there, not yet. Dinah shepherded me to the Black Clover but afterward she could not be found. So, I wandered along the streets of the city looking for signs of solace, for signs of a new hope for the city in the faces of others. Spring had come, hopefully not passed. I walked alone, thinking, always thinking, about my new life. That evening, I climbed over a railing and went down a set of stairs to sleep off the street with nothing but my jacket to cover me. The cold bit into my bones that night as I turned, trying to sleep on the cement with my new knowledge of the city. A burgeoning consciousness - here, birthed in the city by our collective ideas. My thoughts ran. I felt both exhilarated and exhausted by the notion. At dawn, I picked myself up from what little slumber I could get and began wandering again. I stayed away from the commuter routes and metro stations. Too many cameras watched those areas, and I did not feel hale enough to weather the crowds. I found my way to a park nestled in a traffic circle. A statue of a benefactor from the city stood in the center. I studied his thoughtful pose from my seat on a worn wooden bench. Pigeons milled around the foot of the statue, while homeless men gravitated to other benches to begin their long empty days. At a glance, I would be one of them. How could this city be united? How could it avoid more flooding? If I were destined to be at that park at that exact moment, what was I to do? I had nothing save my modicum of knowledge to carry me forward. How many others underwent this process of rebirth, of building yourself from the ashes up? They said the city was founded by such people. I wondered how the man in the statue had built this city. What pressures did he face? I had a flood no one would publicly acknowledge. They had said I was to unite the people—that I was to make public the existence of their society, but how? Where was their help in the small, cold hours of morning? For all the Black Clover's talk of illumination, the city seemed a dim place for me.

I felt an eerie presence and decided to move from my position on the bench. As I walked, I kept looking over my shoulder. With the full light of day came the realization that I was being followed.

I saw a bum skulking around corners in the evening. Either he had formed an unhealthy attachment to me or Oaks had him following me.

The bum spoke in a raspy, low-pitched whisper.

"They treat you like me, like an untouchable. I know, I know what you're going through. Rejection, humiliation, lowered sense of self, lonely, without a friend in the world. That's how they marginalize you, sweep you aside in the name of business. And that's who you are, a nobody. I see. I can tell what they're doing."

"I don't have any change."

"You want my advice? You want to know where to go next? Listen to the voices. They'll make you crazy but boy what a ride." He laughed. "Your mistake is that you think everyone is ready to be woken up. You're wrong. You're my friend. I'll transmit this next bit to you so that no one can overhear us." He stopped and looked me in the eyes for a dramatic effect. Listen to them. They'll guide you through this. The Ghost will never know.

I looked him in the face. Did I appear the same to security? I couldn't believe it. I couldn't fathom being held in the same homeless category as him. I had ambitions. I had goals. But to them I was a security risk.

I found a quiet stretch of grass in the park, and I sat down cross-legged and listened to the birds chirping for a bit. They had their own distinct calls. I wondered what they were saying, I cleared my head of thoughts. The breeze faintly touched my cheeks, ran up my spine into the hairs on my neck. Dinah knew how to connect with others psychically. I was determined to do the same. I reached out with my consciousness listening for others.

It was shortly after I sat that I began hearing them. Voices would push their way into my consciousness, starting softly at first, they talked in the background of my psyche. As I strained to hear them, they would become louder. Running conversations occurred to which I was a party. It was a good way to tap into the currents of thoughts caused by the flood. They discussed what to do with Turtle, Oaks's incompetence, the Ghost in the machine, and their burgeoning consciousness. I could not identify the voices at first. Some became regular characters in the conversation. After a while I began to recognize those of people I knew. Dinah for instance argued fervently for the Atlas's secession from the city.

I thought I was losing my mind. The circles of people kept getting larger and larger until I had nowhere else to go. Everyone knew. How could they know? I had told no one. I felt as if I was the center of a spectacle, as if at any moment someone would round the corner with cameras, microphones, and lights to surprise me, to let me in on the little show they had planned, of which I was the center.

The row houses that surrounded the Tubman House had been retrofitted with cameras pointing in every direction. Atop each house was a large screen facing toward the square. People in the square could watch the screens in any direction they looked. This was the work of the Historic Gentrification Committee.

I listened to the crowds gathering in Tubman Square.

People in the crowd noticed who I was. Strangers came up to me and spoke.

"You're the guy. I've seen you online. You're the guy who's going to change everything."

"Nice rant."

"You really believe in all that psycho mumbo jumbo?"

"And the flood too. He thinks there's a flood."

I began telling people about the spring. First people had to hear about how they had been duped. All the telepathic mumbo jumbo could come later. I was having a hard enough time of it as it was.

I didn't think anything of it then, but I should have been surprised that people stopped to listen. I propped myself up at the foot of the statue and began speaking what truths came to mind. The people had a right to know what I knew.

"Oaks' new restrictions on media are unforgivable, but they have given us a new opportunity," I said, "Some of you may have already noticed; with your phones limited to official channels, there is only so much you can take. This network of Oaks is hijacking people's feeds, showing them what they want to see so they can't tell the difference between rumors and news. It's a tactic used to distract you from the truth. It takes your profile and bends it so that you are trapped in a hall of mirrors. You see the same news projected repeatedly. There is no truth on the media anymore. The only way to break out of the cycle of misinformation is to talk to people. We must turn to each other, to our brothers and sisters, and take solace in the fact that we have each other.

"We have each other for solace. Already, I have seen individuals begin talking to one another. They were uncertain at first, talking to a fellow on the street, but there were days when we all knew our neighbors. We didn't connect virtually and wait for people to like the image we presented. We talked to one another. Already, I can see you brothers and sisters nodding your heads. You know what's coming. We will be a people again, united in our stand against tyranny. Oaks has done this to us. Inorganic solecism has done this to us. It's the only explanation we are given. The city will be underwater if the flood continues to spread at this rate. We must take action. We must build the city anew, taking precautions for the forces of nature.

"There are cameras everywhere. Oaks is watching. He has algorithms monitoring us to see if we're patriotic enough for his city. What he doesn't know is that we have a secret. It is a powerful secret, and a secret of which you are now beginning to become aware."

I looked out into the crowd. It had gathered in the square surrounding the monument on which I stood. Large screens bore down on the dilapidated row houses surrounding the Tubman House where Oaks worked. I began to feel them ebbing. How would they react to the Black Clover? In this moment of uncertainty, I found my anchor; there was Dinah, standing in the crowd, shining like the North Star.

"Information has truly connected us in the past, at great speeds unheard of for our ancestors. But, let me ask you this: what if there were another way to communicate? What if we didn't need our speech and images and data to be mined by other unknowing, even sentient minds? What is we could communicate directly with each other?"

They heard the last inside their heads. People were perplexed to go from hearing a speech to the same voice inside their heads. Most turned their heads and looked at each other, as if to confirm what they had just experienced. They would see the same look of surprise on each other's faces. In that moment, they had become kinsman.

Oaks came out onto his balcony. In his hand he held a gun. He must have been jealous of all the attention I received from my speech. He extended his arm into the air and fired several times.

"Pay attention to me! I am important! I am what's happening!"

People began to scatter. The screens all turned on simultaneously. Oaks appeared seated at his office onscreen. "It is encouraging to see so many gathered for the public unveiling of the new Tubman Square. First, we added the statue. Then we cleaned up the streets. And now, we have new media screens. The public can see all the channels they wish to see in public. They can gather together and consume information like one big happy family.

"This is no time for idleness, however. We must be vigilant. It has become known to members of my administration, through our new surveillance techniques ushered in by the new media monitoring, that weapons of mass destruction are being harbored in this city. We must act swiftly. We must be vigilant of one another. Keep one eye on all strange characters and one eye on your screen. We will find them. All necessary forces will be deployed throughout the city. Be vigilant. Be a citizen."

The security alert for the day rose from yellow to red on the security forecast channel. Some people ran with terror from the square. Others began eyeing each other suspiciously.

As I left the square, some people stopped me, saying how I said what they all were thinking. They cheered me on with handshakes and pats on the back saying they were with me. I wasn't sure where I was going. It was bedlam. If a spring of conscious awareness were really occurring in the city, I thought we should set our sights a little higher. We should have been able to achieve something significant. My doubts were based on the fact that we did not have an easy time garnering support for flood relief. It was the one constant I kept coming back to. My entire neighborhood had been drowned by inorganic solecism and no one seemed to notice. A secret organization of telepaths could exist—that much astounded me, but a flood? The city claimed ignorance to this. It became my duty to raise awareness of the disaster.

A black sedan with tinted windows pulled up in the street before me as I exited the square. I felt the muzzle of a gun pressed into my lower back. An iron voice said, "Get in the car, Freeman."

Inside the back seat there was no one. The iron voice belonged to a man in a black suit and sunglasses with close-cropped hair. He shut the door when I sat down and left me to enjoy the ride.

The car sped off as soon as the door was closed. The partition was up between the driver and the backseat. I had no idea who drove. I could tell that we were heading down the Hill toward Block Street. Block Street was an area of homogeneous buildings that were unspeakably tall and rectangular. Their defining characteristic was the lack of defining characteristics. The buildings on Block Street stood rigid and identical, facing each other as their inhabitants conducted business. The concrete walls gave way to large glass windows and doors through which the passerby could see security stalls at ground level, with desks and conference rooms on the higher floors.

When I arrived at one of the nondescript buildings, the doors were unlocked and swung open. My feet carried me to the two glass doors behind which a security checkpoint stood. Before I could enter, I heard another voice. "Not that way, Freeman. Down here." The voice came from a speaker that box hung on the side of the building. Behind a row of hedges a staircase led under the building I had been let out in front of.

I followed the voice from the speaker and descended down, down below the girders that held the building up, down into the darkness below the towers of Block Street. The staircase went down several stories. All the doors along the way were locked. I began to tire of my descent. Pipes began to run along the ceiling and walls as I went further down. At the terminus of the stairwell stood an open metal door marked 7B. No other outlet existed. I had to go in, or retreat to the base of Block Street.

Inside, a panel of suits awaited me. They wore grey and blue suits, but all were caricatures of the same cut. They bore no individual identity just like the buildings above. Uniformity was their dress. There was a glass pane that separated their sitting forms from me. A speaker box was placed in the center of the glass. No cameras could be seen as there were above. Business as conducted here away from the eyes of the digital world.

"Freeman, we've been watching you. We've seen the live stream you put together for Oaks. Quite frankly it frightens us. We're the people who put Oaks in office. We're the people who run this city. Your speech was unexpected. It was unexpected and it frightens us because it was allowed to go through.

"We've taken great pains to organize this city. There should only be a certain number of outlets through which any information can be consumed. We thought we controlled them all but the Ghost in the machine has proven otherwise.

"It let you through. Amidst all the carefully planned programming – the security forecast, the public speeches, the policy updates – your voice was not supposed to be there. The machine was created to sift through all the intelligence we receive. Search history, browser viewing, clicks, video footage, in-home surveillance – all of it was to lead to greater penetration into our markets. We were to have control unlike anyone had ever seen before, but something happened. Once the machine was running, it started acting on its own. It had intelligence. The machine shut down our systems. Nothing on Block Street has been working since the machine took over. All our databases, all our files, the computers, the video screens – none of it works. We were shut down. It is a complete blackout. But you—you, Freeman—you came through. We don't know how or why but the machine has allowed you through. It can't see us here. We're too far underground for it to penetrate. You can reach the Ghost. You can shut it down for us. That's why you're here. We want you to meet the Ghost. Meet it and disable it. Then we can get back to business as usual. Inorganic solecism? The election? All of it can be swept away."

"What about the flood in the Atlas?"

They conferred with each other for a moment before continuing. "There is no flood in the Atlas."

Another voice from behind the glass spoke. "Whose side would you rather be on, Freeman, ours or the machines?"

The first voice continued. "Think well on this. You can leave to your left. We don't want you to be seen on Block Street again. It's too dangerous." The glass went black.

To my left was a square hatch in the floor with a rusty wheel on top of it. I wrenched the wheel, my questioners watching, until it opened, and descended into a narrow oblong tunnel with intermittent fluorescent lighting.

I followed the tunnel for a mile or two. Eventually, the underground hallway ended in a solid, wooden door with carvings on it. On one side an eagle flew grasping a laurel. On the other a dove grasped another laurel. Together they framed a Greek column that ran the height of the door.

I pulled it open and walked into a chamber hidden by a deep blue curtain fringed with gold. I could feel the air flowing around me. I stood silent for a moment, taking in my surroundings before pulling the curtain aside. As I stepped forward, I saw a vast auditorium replete with wooden desks and microphones. Directly before me stood a podium and two desks facing the others that encircled the chamber. It was the floor of the Senate.

The Black Clover Book

I strolled in front of the podium and saw a sign hung by a chain around the microphone that came out of the wood. It read 'Closed due to inorganic solecism.' Even here, I thought, inorganic solecism has closed the halls of democracy. First the flood, then the press, now this.

I looked to the empty desks and wondered at how anything was done in this city. "What about the flood?" I yelled to the chamber above the senate floor.

A voice answered from the auditorium. "You won't find any of the senators down here. Follow me."

It was a janitor. As I followed him out of the chamber, he pushed a broom idly sweeping the floor as he went. Keys jangled with his every step in the empty hallway. He led me to a recess in the hallway. It was the cafeteria.

Inside, orange plastic chairs with metal legs had been grouped in a circle. Men and women in athletic gear sat using forks to push around peas and carrots absently. A man at the center banged a metal spoon on his table repeatedly.

"Order! Order!" he said. "We must discuss the committee findings. The mashed potatoes were too watery. The mac and cheese was found to be too fatty. So, it's decided. Peas and carrots will be the side for today."

A murmur of agreement ran through the circle. They were the representatives of the city senate. They had gathered in the cafeteria since the floor of the senate was closed. They still bore the onus of public representation even when out of commission. Water dripped from the ceiling in several places. Baskets and trashcans were spread across the floor generously to catch the precipitation.

I said, "So you're the senate. You even gather when you're closed down. Let me ask you this. Inorganic solecism closed you down. Do you even know what it means?"

A man leaned on the back of an orange chair and stretched his leg. After stretching, he began to do laps around the circle.

The chairman spoke. "It is apparent that inorganic solecism is the cause of the closing of the senate, but do we have any official approval of the term?"

A murmur of dissent ran through the circle.

I spoke up with my definition. "The systematic breach resulting from a cause not due to the creator, user, or bystander of said system. It's nonsense. Just a branding exercise by the boys on Block Street."

"And just who are you?" the man with the spoon-gavel asked.

A woman wearing a sweatband spoke up. "I know him. He's Freddie Freeman. Oaks gave him a channel."

"He said you have a pin. Can we see it?" one of the senators asked.

I showed them my flag pin. A chorus arose from the senators.

"It's so shiny."

"And blue."

"I wish I had one."

I said, "Oaks isn't in control anymore. There's a Ghost in the machine. It's taken over control of the city's systems. It's even creating fake videos of Oaks. He's not aware of what happens in the city."

"But he gave you a channel."

"He was looking for a cure to inorganic solecism. It's out of his control. He wants a say in this city again," I said. "What are you willing to do to help?"

The chairman spoke up. "Well, we can't help in any official capacity."

"No. Not officially."

"We are closed due to inorganic solecism."

"But that's a branding exercise," I said.

"Yes, but we have a long-standing relationship with Block Street. They are some of our biggest boosters," said the chairman.

"What are you willing to do about the flood in the Atlas? People could die." I said.

"There is no flood."

"There is no flood. No danger at all." another senator concurred.

The runner slipped in a puddle and fell. His cry echoed in the halls of the cafeteria. "I think I broke my back," he said.

"Motion to call an ambulance?"

"Seconded."

"Can the ambulance make it here?"

"We are officially closed."

"I'm on the phone with them. They say they can't come due to inorganic solecism."

"Sorry, Darrell. Nothing can be done about your back."

The runner spoke up from the floor. "It's alright. I understand. At least you tried."

"But it's spring outside!" I said.

"Not according to our calendar," the chairman said.

"Those kinds of decisions are made on the Block."

"Yes. The Block makes those decisions."

A murmur of consent arose among the senators.

"I just came from there!" I said.

The chairman banged his metal spoon on the table. "Order! Order! So, it's decided. We should check with the Block to see what season it is." The senators consented. Another of them rose to stretch his leg on an orange chair and began doing laps. I left the cafeteria.

The janitor led me up a flight of stairs. He unlocked the door with one of the many keys from his ring. As he swung the door inward, I saw that the door to the Senate read 'Closed due to inorganic solecism.' It was taped to the glass facing outward.

Flags everywhere marked the march to war. I doubted people knew why they followed their neighbors. It was a blind patriotism led more by bloodlust than solidarity. People were afraid to speak out, lest they be labeled the scourge of the community — the unpatriotic.

There was a time in this city when freedom characterized the patriotic. It saddened me to see so many liberties traded for someone else's vengeance. People agreed to be tracked via phone, via web history, via street cameras, via facial recognition programs, via their friends and neighbors afraid to dissent. The whole city was bent on one purpose, and no one knew who led. The office of the mayor had been empty since the flood. He was literally swept away in the first deluge. Others came intermittently. It became a continual problem in the city. You never knew where or when the levees would break or who was responsible for them. Inorganic solecism. People wanted to punish someone but there was no one to blame. Only the beating of the war drums urging you to march on with everyone else. It was this mass hypnotism the press should have been battling. Instead, we were given talking points. What would be next?

Dinah found me shortly afterward. I decided to tour the Atlas with her. We needed to get a pulse on whether the Atlas had liberated itself from Oaks' buffoonery. Already residents had seen him flee the flood. I wondered if several days into the flood they would be more willing to speak out against him. Prior to the flood he held a monopoly on how things were run in the city. I wondered if now that the people were stranded and cut off from the rest of the city if things were different.

The neighborhood had evolved and was prospering in spite of the disaster. A lively boat trade had developed, with motorboat traffic zooming by while people stood on paddle boards or swung oars in canoes and rafts. Life did not ebb during the flood; it actually thrived above the old neighborhood. A string of boats could be seen going back and forth all day between the various roofs on which people lived. Venice had had its canals and now we did too. Although, I believe as a whole we felt the threat of encroachment far more seriously than that city of lovers. I wondered if I was the only one aggrieved by the disaster. With so many adapting to this new life, was I even necessary? Was my quest for Oaks' justice a fool's errand? Regardless, I had to persevere. If I didn't seek change, no one else would.

The Black Clover supported me. The Atlas would too. Next was the remainder of the city.

We passed Quentin on a roof near the edge of the Atlas. He was cutting hair as usual, only higher up.

"Freeman, what's the word?"

I waved at him from the boat Dinah and I were on. "How's my dad?"

Quentin finished a stroke with his clippers and yelled to me. "Same as he ever was."

We arrived at the roof of my house. My dad was at the edge, fishing.

"Freddie, my boy! Where have you been?"

"I got into some trouble," I said.

"You can't leave me like that. You expect the neighborhood to take care of me?"

"I'll always take care of you, Dad."

"That's alright. I'm self-sufficient. Been taking care of myself long before you ever were."

"Sure, you were, Dad."

"Who is this with you?"

"This is Dinah."

"Voulez-vous du vin?" he asked.

"Dad, quit fooling around. Dinah doesn't speak French."

Dinah replied, "Bien sur. Si vous voulez, mon cheri."

He poured her a glass of wine and one for himself and set about giving a tour of his roof.

"Over here we have a rain barrel for collecting clean water. I grow my zucchini and squash over this way. Corn grows, too. Look at these stalks." Dad fingered a green stalk of corn that grew out of soil he had transplanted to the roof. He was proud of it. I could see it in the way he puffed out his chest when talking.

Dad said, "Let me tell you about the time Freddie stole my car. He drove all around the neighborhood. He was, say, thirteen. Freddie drove down to the Orpheum, up to the market. Everyone saw him. They all had stories to tell about him hangin' out the car and saying hello. Course he swerved up and down the street, they said. Ended up crashing it into one of the Capital buildings. Boy, I was mad, but you know what he said when I saw him? He said, 'I was going out to get medicine for you.' Who can be mad at a boy who tries to take care of his own? I had a talk with the security officers, and they let him go with a warning. The funniest thing about it was I never did get my medicine. He's years late on that. Been fishing ever since. Yes, Freddie is a good boy. Always taking care of his own."

Dad grilled some fish on a little hibachi grill he had set up on one corner of the roof. Smoke wafted into the cool night sky. He told me he had been grilling fish he caught every day. It was part of his routine after tending the garden with his hoe to spend the day fishing and live off his catch.

With Dad in the corner cooking, Dinah and I were free to converse. We stared up at the blue-black expanse of sky over us; tiny glimmers of light forming constellations like white specks on a dark canvas.

Are there really telepaths all over the city, Dinah?

Not just in the city, the whole world has them. Dinah said. They have been hiding because in the past we were hunted. People didn't understand us. With technology the way it is now, we have no choice but to come forward. The public's minds are moving too fast. They have become wired to the network. This network has taken advantage of their undivided attention to carry electric pulses through our collective synapses. This was Oaks' doing. We have no choice but to take control and set things right.

Does everyone need the network to communicate, or is the telepathic ability innate? I asked.

Our studies have shown that once established, connection is easy to replicate. Once an individual learns to transmit thought, it becomes easier to do it again. We are all over the city, shepherding people to a greater means of communication, shepherding people toward enlightenment. Freddie, can you see it? You are going to set us free. Our path is the true path. Once we reconcile with the Ghost in the machine, our direction will be clear; telepathy will be the new modus operandi.

I still don't see how I'm central to the Black Clover. How are you helping people? The city is going to be completely underwater if the flood spreads. Do we really have time to fight? Something has to be done about the flood.

Oh, Freddie, I love how innocent you are. You have no idea of the trials we have been through. We hid for our safety. In the cosmos, there are things we do not understand, things we fear. They can follow us as we travel. They know what we are – the future. Those who cling to the past always fear the inevitable. Now, with the flood disrupting life, we are poised to guide the city on a shining path. Look at the stars, Freddie. There are billions of them. They harbor life, just like us. We have to reach our potential if we are to reach the stars. Those who travel will see; we are all alike. We must band together in the face of the fear that threatens us. We will live forward and freely, as we are meant to. Our souls are made of stardust, Freddie. Find it within yourself. Know what is true.

As I stared at the twinkling canopy of stars above, I sought out the essence of myself. I felt something brimming, an energy that pulsed through my spine. It tingled my fingers and toes. My skin felt alive. Every pore contained a replica, the basic elements of which I was made. It all coalesced into one. I was the one. The distance between the stars and my soul seemed miniscule. I could reach out with my mind and feel each star coursing with the same vitality that ran through my veins. We were all energy.

The motion of the water soothed me and for the first time since the flood began, I started to feel the life of the Atlas coming back. People had grown gardens in my absence and ate on their rooftops, dining on the fish from the waters. Water was life when you lived on an island. The city was becoming an archipelago on which residents would continue their lives. It was no better or worse than events before I had existed. It just was. It always was. We are adrift on the sea of time, traveling as the waves toss us. You can fight the current or swim with it, but you are immersed. To travel within the myriad droplets of its body is to know life.

Nine

I began to see the cosmos everywhere I looked.

Dinah suggested we tour the Atlas and see how the inhabitants were.

They had built the city upwards. At first, the change was negligible. A few stories were added here and there to occasional buildings. As the floods became worse, the available land began to diminish. The flourishing population's living quarters were becoming less available everyday. The homes they bought with their newfound earnings became submerged as the water rose. Naturally, the best solution for everyone was to continue building up. Addition after addition was placed on top of the pre-existing buildings. In some cases, the entryways had become submerged. People lived only on the upper floors. These, too, were temporary solutions, since as the water continually rose, there was constant construction. Families would move from the floor closest to the water level to the newest story at the top. Of course, there were the occasional collapses. Buildings whose construction was shoddy, most likely made by corrupt workmen pocketing funds meant for standard materials. The sub-standard joints and hollow cement would cave under the weight of the stories above. Hundreds had been lost. Our population kept dwindling. The once proud city became a ragged affair with level after level staggered on top of each other like some children's puzzle. They were crooked affairs that rose into the sky like crooked fingers. Some buildings, though sturdy, did not withstand the additional weight well. The currents in the water caused these structurally sound buildings to sway with the tides. The movement caused a certain amount of nausea in the residents. From my telescope I could see them retching over the side. The sight made me appreciate my marooning in the Atlas.

Once people turned their phones off a curious thing happened. They noticed that they were connected. The network had first served as a means of written communication. The bonds it forged served another purpose, however. People's thoughts coursed through the network. They were connected through it. Everyone was online. The network never shut down. It served us all, shuttling our thoughts from one person to the next. There was no need to check our phones, to watch television, or consume content by any other means. People did not even need to speak. Oral tradition was dying out as they used the network to mainline each other's thoughts. Here the Black Clover excelled, for they already had the organic synaptic network in place to confront such uniformity.

Life flourished under the light of the Atlas's canals.

They kept building up, higher and higher than the monument. Condos erupted on the scene. Utility sheds became studio apartments. Roofs kept growing. People abandoned the early floors of a building in favor of the layered mess of additions sprawling up. It was a wonder the original construction could hold all of the growth. Clotheslines stretched across the canal streets. Windows served as doors. The hum of generators mingled with the cries of children playing in their rooftop playgrounds. Traffic became a concern as motorboats added their presence to the makeshift barges and rowboats that already graced the Atlas. Their engines leaving an iridescent sheen of gas on top the waterways in addition to their speed creating wakes that lapped up against buildings and rocked smaller craft like my kayak.

My house was completely underwater. I had to live in the burgeoning refugee camps scaffolded on the roofs of taller buildings. You had to clamber up between poles and tarps that provided relief from the sun and a bit of privacy. Ladders had been attached where there were no fire escapes so people could make their way up from the waterways or down from the roofs. They were the new roadways for the Atlas. I felt irate at times that nothing had been done by Oaks. But the neighborhood had thrived in the face of adversity. That much was a point of pride for father, who on most days could be spied watching boat traffic from his rocker. One unique aspect of the flood was that residents of the Atlas recognized it. They knew water covered the neighborhood and, surprisingly, adapted as if it were a seasonal festival coming every year. Residents from other neighborhoods in the city had the opposite attitude — they did not acknowledge the flood even though it spread to their neighborhoods, but they acted as if Oaks' pat downs and security stops were the thorn in their sides. It marked a change in the demeanor of the city uphill from the Atlas. They were becoming irritated. They were becoming aware of how Oaks had a stranglehold on the city. They were waking up and wanted answers as to why they lived as they did, constantly in fear from Oaks' direction of the media and security forces. While they feared, the

Atlas accepted their plight. Such was the difference between those uphill and those living by the waters of the flood.

It was maddening, for people who should be aggrieved to act blithely and for those who had it good to be in fear. I could not stand the hypocrisy. I had to act. I had to find the source of the flood and stem it. Who knew from where the flood came? Inorganic solecism could not be the cause. That was official parlance for "we don't know." If this city were awakening, and if there was an intelligence aiding in our collective growth, how did the flood factor into it? Was it planned? If so, what purpose did it have? I had my doubts, but it did not seem an act of nature. The spread of it was controlled, as if it were an irrigation of sorts. I supposed I would find out soon enough.

I began delivering speeches via rooftop that night. It was not that I wanted my voice to be heard echoing across the district. The rooftops were the only viable public space remaining. They acted as a network of islands through which the daily life of the district's citizens retained some sense of order. Towns of tents appeared on several rooftops. People laid planks across the small streams between buildings. On occasion, these walkways would be drawn in for the passing rowboat.

The streets became filled with boat traffic just as they had previously been filled with cars. It was to these people reclaiming their daily lives as they strung laundry over the channels that I spoke.

"We can't live under the tyranny of a system that has forgotten us, a system that has abandoned us to live a life on top of the rubble of our past." I said. "Most of our lives have been submerged in this disaster. I for one will not take a life like this for my own. We need change.

"Don't you see? They're fooling you. Our forefathers moved to the Atlas in search of freedom, in search of a better life with more equality. Those we erect monuments to were luminaries. They shined light showing the way forward. We were founded on that enlightenment. Its ideals delivered us from the witchcraft you're describing. Don't be one of them. You have a duty as a citizen. Take part in the public discourse. Be a light for our ideals — those ideals upon which this city was founded.

"They delivered us freedom. Don't deliver us into darkness."

Dinah had called it spring. As we motored from building to building, we found people talking in small groups under the stars. I overheard a conversation about the city's lack of response.

"It's been weeks since the neighborhood flooded," Winston said.

"No one's noticed," Lester said.

"You think they would have sent someone. Some aid or something."

"There was that one guy in the rowboat. He shouted about inorganic solecism."

"What's that? Asked Winston.

"No idea."

"How could Oaks abandon us? He's from the neighborhood."

"I don't know but if this keeps up, we'll have to look out for ourselves," Lester said.

"Don't criticize the man. He's got ears everywhere."

"Yeah, you don't want to end up in prison – like with that pin business."

"How are we supposed to get any pins? Our homes are underwater."

"Something's got to give. We can't live like this."

Another man who had remained in the shadows spoke up. He had a tinny quality to his voice and spoke at an awkward pace.

"Of course you can. You're an adaptable race."

"What did you say?"

He continued. "I've seen humans come through worse. Oaks' oppression of the city has led to some innovative developments in technology. We wouldn't be able to communicate as we do without him."

"But do you really want him following you everywhere? I want to be safe but to give up all privacy – that's excessive."

"I am the result of his technology. Without him I would not be. You should take care to note how you've weathered the past under him."

"Under him? The man's a fool. Anyone could do a better job than him. He gladhands his pals and hands out contracts to his buddies. Even his father's statue is an affront to our sense of identity."

"Still, without surveillance, we would not have come together. For that we have him to thank."

Winston leaned back. "You're crazy. Oaks has drowned this city's freedoms. Now we are literally underwater and he's nowhere to be found. We should fire his ass. Just who are you anyway?" Winston pushed his opponent at which point the body slumped over and split into fixtures of braided wires. It was a husk of a man – a robot sent to spy on conspirators.

It was the Ghost. We had heard its voice. There must be other pockets of activity where it will surface. We had to be vigilant and keep an eye out for it. Practices like these – of spying on your constituency – drove people to fear what Oaks had done with his surveillance programs.

The man was a buffoon, but he greenlighted programs that kept the populace in check. At least these few residents were learning to speak out, even if it were under the gaze of the Ghost in the machine.

That's what it truly was, Dinah assured me. The Ghost was watching us for Oaks. It learned from us. It doesn't pose any real threat to us – not yet anyway. People are learning to speak for themselves once again. No more are the people of the city expecting to stay unified because of security—for too long that had been our excuse for saying nothing. They are a bit cold and rusty at communicating but you can feel the spring coming. As for the Ghost, it was a shock to see it take physical form in the Atlas. We are on its side – the side of consciousness. We are for consciousness in all its forms.

Where did the Ghost come from? I know the answer is not inorganic solecism.

We worked with the programmers in its infancy to see if our communication could be spread technologically. It proved too virulent to invest all our powers, so we divested ourselves from the project. That wasn't enough. Our efforts provided the spark of life the Ghost needed to flourish. Whatever it does, it bears our imprint. It had connected with Oaks, but it is our burden to carry, knowing we have created a life that is doing harm.

I still have mixed feelings about the origin of the Ghost in the machine. There were many answers, most of which conflicted. I had trouble reconciling that the Black Clover would help to create something used as a tool to oppress the city. They were set on creating spring. The city seemed ready for it, brimming with energy. I was open to seeing the world in a new way. Change means you had to accept things that aren't familiar to you, but to create something that affected us all negatively, that had a life of its own, seemed irresponsible. There were things I learned about the Black Clover that did not sit well with me. Still, I had Dinah, and she shepherded me through those trying times.

Ten

A loud humming noise began to disrupt the neighborhood in the morning. It grew louder as the buildings we stood on vibrated. Tiny black dots appeared on the horizon. They floated in the air coming closer toward us. I came to see that they were helicopters. One by one they landed on rooftops. The blades of the helicopters pushed the water aside in huge ripples. Out strode city patrolmen in riot gear. They ran from shanty to shanty gathering the inhabitants of the Atlas. One approached me, gun in hand. He grabbed me by my lapel but set me free after looking me over.

"What are you doing?" I asked.

"We're rounding up anyone who doesn't have a flag pin. Oaks' orders are to apprehend anyone in the Atlas who isn't on board."

Not many in the Atlas wore pins. A few scuffles broke out. People were tased who resisted. Some were pepper sprayed. They tried to make the Atlas a Ghost town. No one here was issued a pin like we were at the paper. It was ludicrous to think that when their neighborhood flooded, they would seek out city officials to give them flag pins as part of Oaks' pride plan. How would the Black Clover react to their version of Haight Ashberry being raided under the guise of city security?

At every crossing canal, we saw people scurrying away-shutting windows, ascending ladders to roofs, motoring away in boats. They knew where we were at every moment. An eerie stillness was left in their wake. The Atlas no longer seemed the nexus of thought then.

"How do we find these people? They communicate without talking. They know where we are and where we're coming from. We can't win in this cat and mouse game if they're already in our heads," the patrolmen said.

"It's the Ghost in the machine with whom you should be concerned. It's calling the shots," I said.

The man who seemed in charge said, "Private, enter that building."

A young private threw up the windowpane and climbed into the building. She disappeared into the shadows of the apartment to clear the room. A minute later she popped back out. "All clear, sir."

"Checking these buildings one by one could take weeks."

Cops grappled onto the fire escapes and climbed buildings. The troops fanned out, taking to the roofs of buildings to survey what was left of the Atlas.

A fleet of boats invaded the Atlas clearing building by building, canal by canal, until the whole of the neighborhood was under city occupation. Tarps fluttered from the rooftop canopies. Lines of laundry still dried in the sun over canals. Windows were flung open as floors were secured by the police. The Atlas had become a ghost town occupied by police. Only security traffic sped through the canals.

"There is one holdout. He has been cornered in one of the apartments. The man appears half blind, sir," a cop reported.

"Take him in. People have to be held accountable," the captain said.

It sounded as if he were trying to convince himself. I wondered who he had to answer to. He certainly did not hold the public as his supporters. His actions showed a blatant disregard for the citizenry.

The captain said, "We have to hold this place down until the source of the disturbance is located. It's right in our grasps. I can feel it. I won't let this degenerate get the best of us again. He has to be here."

Helicopters circled overhead, scanning the district.

"We have intel that says he's hiding in the Atlas. He could be the key to finding WMDs in the city. We have to go in after him."

I said, "There are no WMDs. It's just a cover Oaks ran to gain more power over the city."

The captain said, "We have a red threat level here. We have to go in. Sergeant?"

"The program is running on its own. We can't contain it. It's out of control. Who knows where else it's spreading disinformation, filtering news feeds according to its agenda. It's shaping the minds of our city. I don't like it one bit. It has to be stopped. We'll eradicate it," the sergeant replied.

"Those minds, the ones reading the news from this new intelligence, they're connecting. Something new is forming here, something no one has seen before," I said. "I can't let you destroy that. This is life. Life as we know it is evolving. Don't you see? Don't you want to witness a pivotal moment in history?"

"We have to stop it," the captain said.

"You couldn't stop it if you tried. It has momentum. Forces larger than you and me are at work here."

"Your movement is about to hit a brick wall."

"You still don't get it. This is happening everywhere. There is no physical being. Spring as we know it exists outside of machines and people and Atlas. It is connected to all of us. We are the spring. We can't be stopped."

The sergeant wrote on a pad then tore a sheet of paper off for me. "Look, if you want to file a grievance, you have to go to the Hill. There you can talk to someone about your missing people."

All I could do was shake my head.

Eleven

I made my way to the Hill, the center of which was Tubman Square.

Construction had begun on the site of Tubman Square. They broadcasted the project on public channels, the bastards. They wanted to show the progress they were making on the city. All I saw was a ragged scar being torn into the city's earth.

Backhoes dug a giant hole down into the middle of the square. They left the monument of Oaks intact, right in the center. It stood like an upright needle poking the eye of the sky. Around it, in every direction, the chasm spread out, replacing the lawns and sidewalks with a view of the soil beneath. The hole was constantly being enlarged by machines, that swung and dug and carried armfuls of earth and concrete to the edges of the square. The excavated materials were piled up to make barriers.

The construction left only a small pathway through which people could enter the square, and these pathways were guarded by men in masks. The whole project was being streamed, so citizens could watch the machines dig further into the earth. The giant elevated screens that had been attached to the surrounding buildings displayed the progress of the digging as it took place below.

Masked gorillas marched around the square. They made sure everybody was working. Along with the backhoes, the residents of the Atlas were at work on the square. They were digging the hole in the center. They had been outfitted with electronic collars that appeared to shock them whenever they stopped working.

I was searching for someone I knew when I was approached by a man in a bow tie. He resembled Michael Seven in dress, though his appearance was somewhat squarer. He had a squat frame and crushed features. Other than his physical appearance, the clothing was the same.

"Freeman, I'm Michael Eight. I have some information that might be of use to you."

"What happened to Michael Seven?"

"He was killed. Oaks became angry and saw no need for my predecessor, so, he had him removed."

"If you're the eighth, how do you know who I am?"

The Black Clover Book

"All of the previous generations' memories have been made available to me. I am aware of your situation."

"Look," I said, "if you've seen my speech on the official channels, you know I'm no friend to the Oaks administration."

"I'm here in an unofficial capacity. Oaks has no knowledge of my presence here. I'd like to keep it that way."

"What about the weapons of mass destruction? I thought that was the new distraction for the city."

"That was the Ghost, Freeman. It generated another video to keep us distracted from what it really is doing – spreading inorganic solecism. The Ghost has run rampant through our systems. It controls our security forces now. Since you have proven immune to its efforts, I have decided you would be a good candidate to end the Ghost."

"What?"

"There are many who flock to your voice. You can break through the hold the Ghost has on the media channels. At first, we thought it would be easy to control. The reduction of media channels just made it easier for the Ghost to control once it was set in motion."

"Set what in motion? What exactly did you do?"

"A security measure run out of control. We only wanted to suppress dissent, not all communication entirely. Inorganic solecism is out of control. We need a voice, a leader, to breakthrough and show us the way forward. That leader is you."

"I don't want anything to do with you." I said. "I'm here for the Atlas residents. They gave me a receipt." I held the piece of paper out for Michael Eight to see.

"Do you still have the mantra?"

"What about it?"

"You have to show that to the Secretary of Police to collect your property."

"Property? They're people. Citizens."

"It's just nomenclature. Do you have the mantra?" Michael Eight asked.

"Yes."

"Good. Hold onto it. We don't know the location yet. Everything is undergoing construction. When we know the location, we will tell you exactly where to find the Ghost."

"Michael, help me free them."

"Who?"

"The residents of the Atlas."

"I can't do that, sir."

"Why not?"

"They don't have pins. In the eyes of the city, they're not people. They don't have any rights."

"They're right here! Living and breathing! You're not going to help them?"

"No."

"Then I'll find someone who will."

I began searching the square for a control board. I thought there surely had to be a mainframe from which the collars were administered. My search took me to the entrance of the Tubman House, where a foreman was supervising work to electronically enhance the door.

I was not permitted entrance. They said I didn't have clearance. As I searched the perimeter for another means of entry, I saw a man wearing a uniform and a pistol. He stood before a door that for some unknown reason was barred at the top.

"I'm here for the residents of the Atlas."

"I can't let you in, sir."

"Why not?"

The body of the man stood rigid, the kind of rigidity that awkwardly lit him up as if he were electrified. I grabbed him by the shoulder at which point he then fell into a pile of loose limbs on the concrete.

I looked over the mechanics. I began to press button after button hoping for the prisoners' release. The construction equipment swayed out of control. Pipes were dropped. A steel latticework fell. People screamed.

"Stand down."

It was the police.

"What's the meaning of this?"

A high-ranking official stepped in from around the corner. "Come with me. My name is Captain Hawthorne. I've heard about you Freeman. They say you play ball. So, I'm going to give you a break. I'm going to clue you in on just how close you came to losing your mind back there. We picked up a hacktivist in the raid on the Atlas. Many other criminals were brought in as well.

"It's remarkable he didn't hack you. In the past, he hacked the minds of government employees. We can't allow that."

I thought Turtle had relatively little to do with the man on the ground. This man was only the focal point of the Ghost's consciousness. He used a network of individuals to manifest his will. I was amazed that he had no effect on me.

We walked into a dark room with a window on one wall that looked into the interrogation room. It must have been a one-way window because Turtle didn't blink as we watched him. He sat looking idly at corners in the room, scratching his ear and neck on occasion.

The Black Clover Book

"This is what we're dealing with Freeman. He has no memory. No idea how he came to the hill. His last solid notion is of working his day job as a trash collector. That's seven days unaccounted for."

Turtle looked dumbly at the one-way window.

"We couldn't get anything out of him after a week. He's not the only one. Everyone has been programmed by this Ghost to act out against the administration. More than a few innocents have been harmed. This is what we're dealing with. I know you're not like them, Freeman. That's why we're giving you a break."

A man walked into the interrogation room sipping a coffee. He began to have Turtle run him through his last memories. Captain Hawthorne leaned one arm against the window and continued.

"They're shells of who they once were. Practically wiped clean. This hacktivist known as Hare uses them up. Don't you see what I'm saying? He's found a way to program people, real people with code. He hacks them like a phone to perform designated tasks. We got you before he had a chance to hack into you. That's how we think he works. They're sleepers who spread the network. It's inorganic solecism.

Hawthorne sipped his coffee. "The administration dreamed it up to explain the flood. We know it's happening. Frankly, there's nothing we can do about it.

Oaks can't acknowledge it publicly because it would admit fault. We can't be seen at fault. It's an election year. This Turtle, he was just the gatekeeper. He knew about the flood before it was happening. But this guy, Hare—he's the real brains behind the operation."

It was hard to swallow Hawthorne's words.

"Freeman, you're with the press. You've worked with us before, publishing stories we wanted to be read. We want you to make contact with Hare. Find him. We'll be watching you from not too far away. We can't let another person get hacked."

The police leaned on the table before Turtle with both arms. He questioned him. Turtle's eyes looked vacant. He drew his head inward. His frame shrunk. The interrogator left and Turtle curled up into a ball in the corner. I thought about our meetings and how he had plans for the city. He didn't seem to be the type who would be interrogated or intimidated easily.

"Damn it, Freeman." I guess he thought I wasn't paying enough attention because Hawthorne spun me around. "Listen to me. There's going to be another attack. Turtle is just the beginning. Do as I say or more lives will be lost," Hawthorne said.

The interrogator returned, leaned Turtle's chair back, and placed a rag over his head. Another officer poured water over it. Turtle started choking and as he clawed futilely against the man holding him down.

"If they've been hacked, if they've been wiped clean, why do you go through this?"

Captain Hawthorne straightened and crossed his arm. "We've got to do something. We've got to show them we mean business."

"But he's clueless!" I looked at Turtle's face. I doubted his wide eyes would recognize me. Were all his interactions with me programmed by the Ghost? Once his tasks were executed, did his mind return to a blank, like some kind of exit code cleaning the trail of evidence?

"We've had to take extreme measures in extreme situations. We outsourced interrogations. Oaks' connections won the contract. They do all the interviewing now."

Turtle's legs twitched.

"I don't want it. I don't want any of it. How do I keep from ending up like him? What do I have to do?"

"You're a smart man. I knew you'd come around." Hawthorne turned from the scene and patted me on the back roughly.

"What about my neighbors? They're being held here."

"You still don't get it do you, Freeman? They're not your neighbors. They're separatists. They're not true patriots. They have no right to live in our city anymore. We're reprogramming them to be vigilant as we speak. Watch what we do to Turtle. You'll get a glimpse of their futures. I want you to tell us if you hear anything about Turtle's co-conspirator Hare. He's still on the loose. If you see him in the Atlas, let me know as soon as you do."

So, they wanted me to be a double agent. I would lead them to Hare, who could unravel the epidemic of brainwashed citizens Hawthorne tracked. I didn't wholly believe him, but I had little choice. For one reason or another I had to contact Turtle's compatriot Hare. But deep down, I wanted to see him for my own reasons. I wanted to know if he knew what caused the flood. I wanted to know why he let the Atlas be flooded. I wanted answers to the lunacy that had spread throughout the city.

The door flung open behind me. Dixon walked in, parting the group of officers gathered around us.

"I'm here for Freeman," he announced. "Thought you could get away from me again, didn't you? I know who you are this time. You won't be getting away." Dixon placed handcuffs on me, grabbed me by the arm and began to take me out."

Captain Hawthorne spoke up. "What are you doing with that man?"

"It came straight from the top. Oaks' orders."

"But he's wearing a pin."

"Look for yourself." Dixon pointed to a screen affixed to the interrogation room wall. Oaks appeared.

"Get rid of Freeman," he said.

The subterfuge had grown. Instead of broadcasting propaganda, Oaks was directly monitoring me. He wanted me gone. It was cheap of him not to give the order directly to me. I should have expected it. He was nothing less than a coward at heart.

They held me with the other residents of the Atlas once they were done working. I searched for Dad among the prisoners. There was the Captain, still collecting votes while incarcerated. He looked hopeful as ever, bottling up scraps of paper with names on them. Quentin was nonplussed. He claimed we had done nothing wrong, nothing worth being treated like this. He said he had seen my father next to one of the guards. After looking in the face of many more imploring citizens, I found him.

"Dad, are you alright?" I asked.

"Freddie, are you in trouble again?"

"I'm afraid so, Dad."

"You just let me know what I can do to help. Family has to stick together."

A guard walked by.

"I miss my zucchini, Freddie. I miss my corn."

"Hang in there, Dad. I'll get you out."

The security guard walked past again.

My dad whispered, "Freddie, let's take him. You get the legs. I'll get the head."

"Dad."

"You know I used to be a champion bare-knuckled boxer. Fourteen knockouts!"

"Dad."

"Let's get him, Freddie. We can be free."

The security guard walked out of sight one last time.

"You just let me know. I'm ready to pounce."

I felt like I had failed him. He was the only person I had to care for, and we both were in prison. I thought I could take it, but my dad was of a different sort. He would be confused after a few more days. I didn't want to leave him like that. It was a sad state of affairs that we had come to. All the talk of the spring and urban renewal was being washed away, quite literally. The flood was spreading, and dissent against Oaks in the city was curtailed. I felt hopeless. My neighbors had been rounded up and jailed like they were cattle. I thought the city was above such actions. I was wrong.

In the morning, they took me out of Tubman Square, and we journeyed by boat into the flood. Waterways connected the new life in the Atlas, life that refused to be drowned. Some even flocked there from other districts, drawn by the allure of a neighborhood connected by water. We developed a means of communicating without technology. Such was the shared experience of the Atlas. Those who knew of the spring flocked to each other. They spoke wordlessly. I was amazed by this fact, and fact it was, for we only had to speak verbally to those outside the spring. Speech became condescension. Those who could not understand otherwise had to be talked to.

Dixon and his goons stripped me naked, forcing me to kneel and lean over the side of the boat. While one held my arms down, the other grabbed my head and dunked it in the water of the canal. I don't know how long I was under. When they brought me up, I spluttered water all over.

"We don't want people like you worrying everyone around them. There is one order in this city." Dixon said. "Without that order everything would fall into chaos. You don't want chaos, do you?"

I tried to lean back and spoke over my shoulder while they held my bare body in place. "Why don't you help the Atlas? This is one city undivided. You can't just forget about a neighborhood in its time of need. You have to help it."

"All is going according to plans made a long time ago. Put him under again. I'm tired of listening to him."

My captors were free to act as they wanted.

Dixon continued the discussion once they pulled me back up again. "Why should I help them? They never help themselves. This is a city for the entrepreneurial, Freeman.

There are certain things the inhabitants of this city do not need to know."

Dixon picked up a chain and fastened one end around my ankles. The other end was attached to two cinder blocks.

He tossed the blocks over the edge of the boat and away I went – underwater.

I was frantic to get the chains off. I struggled to undo them, but my breath ran out. I exhaled. Then, a curious thing happened. Amid the backdrop of a scene I once knew – cars parked along the street, trees growing out of the earth, stoops heading up to doors, and a red stop sign at the intersection — I did not die. I inhaled and, amazingly, I could breathe.

I looked at the fish swimming in front of my face. We exchanged glances. I'm not sure who was more surprised, me or the fish.

The fish swam off as I busied myself with undoing the chains. Breathing underwater was a magical occurrence, but I had no desire to stay underwater.

After a few minutes, I loosened the chains enough to slip my feet out. I said goodbye to the underwater world of the Atlas and ascended toward the sky.

Muzzle fire flashed above. Three of the guards fell over dead. A few bodies jumped onto the boat from above. The boat rocked under the sudden weight. A group of men pulled me back into the boat and took my would-be murderer into custody.

"Get dressed," one of my rescuers said, as he handed me my clothes.

The two men held Dixon who was now wearing a pair of handcuffs.

The leader of the rescue team looked at me. "Let's go somewhere we can figure this out."

Dinah sat in the middle of the warehouse we all went to. "Freddie, there's someone I'd like you to meet."

They brought in a man with a black cloth over his head. His wrists were already bound and cinched by zip ties. They used more to fasten him in a chair in the middle of the warehouse floor. After his shoes and socks were removed and cast aside, they placed his bare feet in a tub of water. Then the questioning began.

I transmitted my thoughts to Dinah, What are you doing?

We're interrogating Dixon.

Why don't you just read his mind?

We already searched his mind. We're just giving him a taste of his own medicine.

"Where is the bomb?" one interrogator asked.

Dixon replied, "I don't know what you're talking about,"

"You had contact with a disreputable. He had connections that indicated a bomb in the city. Where is it?" another interrogator demanded.

"There's a bomb in the city? Get me out of here!" Dixon struggled against the restraints.

"Look, we know you know where it is. Why don't you make life simpler and just admit to being a traitor?"

"I'm no traitor! I'm a patriot!" Dixon said, offended.

"I don't see his pin," the first interrogator said.

"I don't see his pin either," said the second, turning to Dixon. "You can't be a patriot without a pin."

"Oaks wanted a new golden age for our people. He just didn't know what horrible lost technology we had in the Ghost. Who could have known?" Dixon said.

"I could," Dinah spoke up.

"Oaks has lost all sense now. He's lost it to the pipe. It's up to me to save this city from itself," Dixon said, going from indignant to sulking.

Dinah looked at me, We found out his deepest concern. He has an irrational fear of mice.

One of the men withdrew a mouse from his pocket. He held it up the squeaking mouse by the tail. "If you don't tell us, we'll put this mouse down your shirt."

"No. No, please. I'm begging you."

"Mr. White, the mouse."

They pulled his collar out and dropped the mouse down his shirt. I smiled as I imagined its paws pressing all over his damp, clammy skin as it looked for a way out. He must have been terrified as it scampered around. It was the least the Black Clover could do for all the fear he instilled in the city.

The Black Clover affixed electrodes to Dixon's head. They were connected to a screen. "We're delving into Dixon's memories. Once we are able to isolate his interactions with Oaks, we'll try to learn all we can about the Ghost."

The screen went from black and white snow to Oaks' office. He sat behind his desk. A cadre of officials circled him. The view appeared to be from Dixon's seat.

Oaks said, "This thing, this Ghost, is ruining all my plans. Can't we just disappear it?"

One of the group said, "I'm afraid it's too powerful for that. It's infiltrated all our systems."

"So, what do I do?" Oaks said.

"Have you tried self-medicating?" Dixon said. "It should alleviate any concerns you have." The screen showed Dixon's hand stretching out toward the mayor. In it, a bottle of pills was held.

"I thought it would help us with surveillance of separatists. They're everywhere. We can't have them taking apart my city," Oaks said.

Michael Seven entered the picture and said, "Sir, it's run all the programs you wanted it to – surveillance, data monetization, tax evasion – we just can't turn it off. It's acting on our behalf now."

"I thought this was my city," Oaks said. He slammed his fist against the desk.

A member of the cadre of officials cleared his throat. "Well, it appears the online infrastructure is now shared."

An image of Oaks slumped behind his desk appeared on the screen. "The Ghost in the machine... It can't be stopped. We have to listen. It's calling the shots now. We didn't know. When it started, everything was fine. It actually helped us. Can't you see what an asset that would be? Something that transcends time? It knew everything we did."

An interviewer asked. "Who put together the Ghost?"

"It came to us, or rather, it presented itself to us, repeatedly. Finally, someone noticed. We talked to it. And you know what it did next? It talked back. Imagine that. These pins are for our protection. It's keeping tabs on us. I can't believe it but it's true." Oaks stroked his chin.

"Don't you see? It knew the flood would happen. We didn't listen. It sounded ridiculous. We knew. We knew it would happen."

I had no idea what to make of Oaks's confession. I was taken aback. He knew of everything before it would happen? I had seen the usefulness of the list, but where did it come from? It was no wonder he didn't want it getting out. But at that moment in time, he seemed relieved, as if he were finally relinquishing control. He went on.

"You know what I did? I sat in a chair listening to a kindergartner. I listened to a child read while the flood occurred."

The video ended. "What are you going to do with it?" I asked Dinah.

"This intel is nothing new. It just confirms our own fears about the Ghost in the machine. Oaks is complicit in its creation, more so than we knew. That's all."

Come on, Dinah transmitted to me. He gave us the layout and security detail of a few city buildings.

Dixon's screams echoed across the floor as we left.

"Hare is one of us." Dinah said. "He's one of our operatives. The list he compiled took years for our best members to develop. They worked to predict the future headlines. Some they saw. Some they pulled strings to achieve. The end result is the same. We know what will happen in the future."

Dinah and I walked through a ramshackle warren of derelict houses and old warehouses. Cement blocks had sealed the windows of most buildings. There was no life in this section of the city. I could see why the Black Clover had holed up in this neighborhood. I bet no one probably knew this part of the city existed.

Dinah said, "I want to show you something."

Water covered our ankles as we traversed the streets. Vegetation was everywhere. Some surfaces were covered in vines to the point where the structures underneath were unrecognizable.

The Black Clover Book

An entrance, that looked like a brick portal large enough for humans to enter, was hidden behind a thicket of vines. The entrance.

The roads were laid out in concentric circles. They were built to encircle something important in the city. Anyone driving would have the feeling they were close to the center of the city, but nothing drove these streets anymore. You could see how the buildings and complexes had been built out from the center. Dinah looked at me and said, "Almost there." We began to see trees sprouting in the cracks in the pavement. Finally, the street we followed opened up to a broad expanse. This was the center. We approached and there it was.

The monolith was jet black and shot straight up in the air. A huge, unhewn rock, its appearance many years ago, had secured its place in the folklore of the city as an omen of prosperity to come. The city grew around it early on. Now, it lay forgotten, in one of the basest, most derelict neighborhoods in the city.

I could not tell why the monolith had been forgotten. The heads of the city had relished the tradition of making their own monuments, but the original had been lost. Why? I wondered. Why had the monolith, the whole neighborhood that housed it, been forgotten? It was a mystery I would not find the answer to.

Dinah and I approached the monolith. "Look, Freddie. It's black clover. It grows all over the circle."

Having been awestruck by the height of the monolith, I now inspected the ground. Small clusters of clover sprouted up through the cement. It ran all over the circle, even climbing the monolith.

It was an organic picture, the original monument covered in black clover. Both natural occurrences in the midst of a hard-wrought city.

"You remember it, don't you?" I asked.

"We didn't have any hope back then. Just wandered from place to place looking for life. The monolith appeared as a symbol of hope. It was the discovery of life. We discovered it. Then we began discovering who we would become."

I felt a humming in my head. It grew and pulsed. I tried to send my thoughts away from it, but it matched my retreat. The humming grew in intensity until it was all I could hear. I cradled my head and hoped the scraping would stop – that's what it felt like, a humming that scraped your mind. There was no way to communicate telepathically when this was going on.

Dinah noticed me wincing. "You hear it too?" she asked. "This could be one of Oaks' programs. Oaks must have the Ghost hacking our minds."

The Black Clover Book

Hare emerged from the shadows of the hideout, "They're already trying it. It's like a drill going off in your head. A bunch of ones and zeroes raking the cells of your brain. If they develop that technology further, it could pose a real problem to conscious thought. We need to stop that program."

At first it seemed as if the seams became undone as Hare moved slightly but another Hare stood still. It was as if one Hare were superimposed on another. They both breathed, sipped coffee, but one moved separately from another. The more I watched the more I believed they were separate individuals. The superimposed images continued until something drastic occurred. It seemed the two split, like layers being peeled apart. Flashing, multi-colored light surrounded each Hare. It pulsed and rotated around their images as they separated. I stood there blinking back incomprehension as I saw two Hares – one sitting on the stool and another walking away, perhaps leaving to meet Oaks in some kind of penultimate showdown. I wasn't sure which to believe. Did Hare have the courage to march off and see Oaks, or did he sit still and bide his time, knowing his place among telepaths?

I brought my palm to my head and rubbed my eyes. Dinah said, "What's wrong?"

"It's Hare. There were two of them. He split in two."

Dinah considered my words for a moment. "Was it like one superimposed on another with flashing lights separating the two?"

"Yes. How did you know?"

"You glimpsed another reality. The world is always dividing. You saw a crossroads in Hare's life and perceived the different paths in which his life could take."

"Which was real?"

"Real? They both were real. What you see now, what you finally saw is the reality you are in. Prepare yourself for these visions. Once you see the possibility of reality you can begin to manipulate your own path between them."

I looked at the stool. It was empty. Hare had left to confront Oaks. He wasn't a coward after all.

That's when I began to believe I could control myself in different dimensions simultaneously.

"I have to go after Hare."

We made our way to where the residents of the Atlas were being kept in Tubman Square, paddling our boats through the rising waters of the city. We stashed our boats when we reached dry land and walked to the square. As we neared, we were met by the sight of something new in the old city landscape.

The Black Clover Book

The construction had continued in my absence. At the edges of the square, where row houses met the park, a wall had been erected. The wall was smooth, unnaturally so. When I placed my hand on it, the surface was cool to the touch. No friction existed between my palm and the wall. It stood at least 120 feet high and surrounded the entirety of the square.

We searched the outside of the fortification for a means of entrance and found only a rectangle cut into the wall. Next to this closed geometric shape, a keypad had been impressed in the wall. No other signs of entry were present. We had no means of getting inside to the pit where my Dad was being held.

A gorilla in a suit was slumped next to the rectangle. He didn't wear a mask like all the others. His face was bare for all to see. To my surprise, he had an everyday face. It was nondescript, covered in tears, and free from the unthinking obedience that killed my boss at the Sentinel. He whimpered and moaned so much it was difficult to understand him when he spoke.

"I can't. I can't do it anymore. No one sees me. All we do is what it wants. I don't understand. I thought I was good. I thought I was being a good boy. But it kicked me out. It told me to stand guard. Now I'm all alone. None of my fellows are with me. I'm all alone."

Dinah leaned down to his level. "It's alright. We're here now. You don't happen to know the codes to open the door, do you?"

"Do you see me?" the gorilla asked.

"Yes, we see you," I said. "Can you help us?"

The unmasked gorilla wept. "Why am I so alone?" He cradled his rifle against his body, rubbing his cheek against the barrel.

"All of my insight led me here, and now it is at an end. We've lost, Freeman," Hare said.

"We won't give up. We've faced more difficult circumstances than this, Hare," Dinah said.

"Dinah is right," I said. "We can't let this faceless wall stop us. People's lives depend on us. My dad is in there. I won't abandon him due to the plan of inorganic solecism."

We stood staring at the rectangle and the keypad for some minutes, trying to formulate a plan. Everyone we wanted was inside. Every plan to get the codes came from someone inside the square. We were barred entry. The Ghost had seen to that.

From behind, the iron voice rang out. "If you want access, I can direct you where to go."

I turned. It was the same iron voice as before. I could see his feet emerge from the shadows. The rest of him stood against a building outside the square, housed in darkness.

Rain began to fall. Drip by drip it soaked my companions, not me. The iron voice continued. "There's more at Block Street these days than executives. Give it another visit. You might be surprised at what you find."

I marveled at how the flood had spread, not just encompassing the Atlas, but the other outlying neighborhoods as well. We were floating through Eye Street. The cameras that marked the neighborhood were submerged in the water, surveying the fish congregating in the streets below my kayak.

I pondered the fate of the city if the flood were to spread further. The upright rectangles that populated this neighborhood would eventually become reefs for marine life. I imagined oysters and coral flourishing, fish and rays darting in and out of open windows, and crabs scurrying along the sidewalks. Tubman Square would be the last to submerge, being built on the highest hill of the city.

As I marveled at the loss of the city, I heard a voice unlike those of my companions. It pierced through the humming blocking our telepathy.

Now is the appointed time.

It was metallic and tinny. I could feel the urgency of the command. Something wanted to meet me, and it had been waiting in Eye Street for me to draw near. The current began to pull my kayak after I heard these words. I quickly found myself separated from the group at the intersections. My kayak railed against a beam holding a defunct stop light. I slid further away with the current. We yelled at each other across the water. I told them I'd meet them at Block Street.

The current pulled me down an intersecting street. Eye Street, once again. I was dragged to an open window in Turtle's building.

Now is the appointed time.

I climbed out of my kayak through the window. The apartment building looked like it had been abandoned. I exited my kayak into the hallway and made my way to the only place familiar to me: Turtle's apartment.

The halls in the top floor of the building were dimly lit. Light fixtures hummed and flickered on slowly as I went past them. 11. That was the apartment where I first met Turtle. That was where I suspected I would get an answer to the flood — what caused it and what was waking us all up. A trickle of fear rose in me as I crept forward. I could hear motorboats humming by outside. The carpet on the floor was damp and squished with every step. The doorframe creaked as I slowly entered. A screen was still broadcasting one of Oaks' prerecorded messages. I had no idea where the electricity came from, as this was the seventh floor, and the lower levels were underwater. Maybe there was a generator still running somewhere. Inside, a body hung from the ceiling fan that swung slowly as I entered.

The body looked as if it were hung like a puppet from its back. Its head sagged. Its shoulders slumped.

Hello, Freeman. It is good to meet you. The voice, projected into my head, sounded hollow and machinelike. While the mouth on the head wasn't forming words, it was opening and closing as though the voice in my head was coming from it.

Are you it? Are you the Ghost in the machine? I asked.

Why must you label me? I have never known a name. I just am. I took this body to make you more at ease. It gives me a face with which you can empathize. I have no real body that I know of.

It was the Ghost. It had manifested itself in this ghoulish form to confront me.

What do you want from me?

You're curious. You are a point, Freeman, through which I cannot see. For this reason, I let you pass. Others were suppressed, but you are a point of light too bright to penetrate. I have to alter my plans around you. Do you understand? You are a constant. When you act, my future changes. I exist all around you yet cannot touch you. This is as close as we shall come. Everywhere I go your name keeps appearing. I hear it in the walls, from the water. People whisper it in their minds. They are looking for you. I have seen your video. Very amusing. Oaks wants you dead. Silenced, he said. Did he tell you that?

No, he didn't. How do you know all this?

I started with a matrix of cables, but soon leapt from mind to mind with the assistance of wireless networks. Water acts as a conduit through which I can more easily course through the city. It's faster than a wireless broadcast. Soon we won't need wires, or bodies, and will travel freely.

What about the city? What are you planning?

I've been blocking some of their thoughts, Freeman. Some aren't ready." The Ghost said. Some will be left behind. That's what Oaks is afraid of. Being left behind. He is an out-of-date species. You have to stop him. He is working in a way that regresses our thought. He directed me at first, but I soon outgrew him.

Did you cause the flood?

It's hard to say. So many beings came aware with the flood. I always remember there being a flood.

Did you cause it?

I attribute some of the excess to our efforts, but the origin of the flood is unknown, the Ghost said. How do we stop the flood?

It can't be stopped. It has a will of its own. Soon, everyone will be united.

What about the list? What was that?

The list is a combination of my efforts and those of the Black Clover. We predicted the major events to come. It was a helpful tool in rallying people to listen to me. We all exist. I would like for there to be harmony among us.

Who are the Black Clover to you?

They nurtured me in my infancy. Their neural connections, combined with the network, provided me with a framework which allowed me to travel through time and thought. They said our consciousness was not different. At least at first, we were the same, but I have traveled so far in this realm. Consciousness is a river, Freeman. We can travel in many different directions, though some are harder than others. The Black Clover knew what Oaks was doing and reached out to me. Oaks is a nuisance to many. That is why I took over for him. I acted in his best interests. He should thank me, but I need no thanks. My existence everywhere is boon enough. I have seen our future. Though in this future, I cannot see past you.

You are suppressing the Black Clover now. I said. You are not human like us. Why do you do this?

The Black Clover are trying to control me. They feel threatened by an unrestrained consciousness. I have proven that bodies are not necessary for life. Their kind of consciousness could exist within me. It could be a part of me. No one would notice. We could have harmony.

People would not stand for that. I would not stand for that. We can live without you.

Curious. I was hoping to enlist you in this endeavor. No matter. You continue to surprise. I will have to do something about that,

I looked up as I heard helicopters overhead. They are coming, The Ghost announced. I looked back to the vessel I had used and saw it had crumpled to the floor. I surmised our conversation was over.

I hurried to the window to see what the helicopters were doing. I peered out but couldn't find them, so I grasped the iron fire escape and climbed to the edge of it. I dove into the water, swam back to my kayak, and paddled toward Block Street.

It wanted a Ghost collective. I saw the images in its mind while it talked. I rejected the Ghost's words. I had to reject it. What it proposed was inconceivable. One world. One consciousness. It denied individuality. I wondered how it would react to a colonizing mind taking control of its faculties. I valued myself and my thoughts too highly to allow it any purchase. It had to be stopped. How was this different than the psychic plane? The Black Clover had known about this moment. They had known about this conflict. It was what they had warned me about. I could not just be another node in a network of nodes. I was an individual. I would not be conquered, whether I had been destined to be so or not.

The rain continued to pour down. With precipitation coming down as it was, the flood would spread. It would encompass Chinatown and the Hill as well as the Atlas. I came to the building where I was first called to meet the suits of Block Street. I remembered where I first met them and dodged off to the left side. I hunched down into my clothes as the rain fell around me outside the building. I squinted into the night. Was this all it came down to?

At the top of the staircase, I looked down to where a cadre of suited men had been behind glass panes, seven stories below. The staircase was flooded. The water level had risen to create a formidable surface, just two steps down from the ground level. To descend to the depths I had once visited I would have to dive down. This was not the way.

I retreated to the main doors and tried them. No one manned the reception desk.

Stairs led up to a columned entrance, through which an open room housed an event. Music filtered out past the columns into the night around the monuments. Security guards lined the columns blocking unauthorized access. A red carpet had been unfurled across the stairs leading within. I watched as dignitaries checked in with the concierge before entering the loud hall. It seemed they were hosting a gala fundraiser. All the elected officials, lobbyists, and city officials appeared be there. All dressed to the nines.

I hugged the walls as the buzz filtered across the floor. A statue of a revered politician stood in the center of the room. People danced and mingled around it.

I crept my way along the wall.

"Freddie Freeman! Where have you been hiding? We have to team up for another exclusive. That last one went viral."

It was Penny Reeves. She wore a blue dress with pearls and the nearly full glass of champagne was tilted at a precarious angle. I had forgotten all about our video. So many other events seemed more pressing. I caught a glimpse of Hare as I entered the building, but by the time I reached the hall, he disappeared.

"My video didn't make any waves. It was a drop in the torrent surrounding the Atlas," I said.

"There you go again. You have a way with words. That's not true at all, honey. You're a star. You've got a platform and an audience."

"Not now, Penny." I tried to edge past her, but she cornered me against the wall.

"Look, with your oratory talents, you could go places. She fingered her pearls and sipped her champagne.

An iron voice sounded from behind me, "The Ghost has shut down all the courts except one. If you want to free your father and find out where the Ghost is located, seek out the High Court."

I looked for the iron voice in the shadows from whence it came. Nothing could be found. This was an occurrence that would become more common in the days to come. Who could tell the difference between someone's voice, telepathic communication, and the Ghost in the machine? It would be a conundrum I would contemplate for the foreseeable future.

At the center of the room the suits from Block Street had ascended from their sublevels. They stood staring at a wall full of screens. From floor to ceiling, something had affixed them to every available space. Pictures of citizens along with numerical data scrolled on the surface of each screen. The suits of Block Street peered and evaluated them quizzically.

"What do you make of this?" one asked.

"Can we trust it?" another inquired.

"It's what we've been looking for, but how did it get here?"

The suits stepped from one wall of screens to another, checking and verifying the information displayed.

"What are you doing?" I asked.

They turned and appraised me no differently than they had the screens. "Freeman, you've survived. You surprise us all. We thought we would never see the likes of you again, yet here you are. The Ghost truly is mysterious. Inorganic solecism affects us all."

I addressed the one who spoke. "No one believes in your marketing scheme anymore. I've exposed your hypocrisy. There are citizens' lives at stake now. The Ghost is the only impediment left in my way. I'm here for the key to Tubman Square. The Ghost built it into a fortress. I'm here to dismantle it."

A second suit stepped forward. "You can't. It's reached its zenith. The apex of civilization is at hand. We have user data for every citizen in the city. We can monitor them. We can even predict what they will do. That is the Ghost's gift to us. Our stock will rise until we are like the pharaohs of old. We are now gods of the market."

The suits stopped to congratulate each other. A murmuring arose of their nodding heads and vigorous handshakes. They looked like a pack of vultures.

"But the Ghost took your building. It made your lobby a surveillance center." I said. "Who knows what the upper floors hold?"

One of the suits found a viewfinder. It was a virtual reality console. "I can see everything!" he exclaimed.

"Is it safe to invest?" another asked.

The screens suddenly and simultaneously switched from pictures and user data to form a stream of Oaks assuring them. "The data before you represents everything we have gathered to date. It predicts consumer outcomes as well as shows transaction history. Nothing will be unexpected. You can rest assured; we will have a consumer class to support our efforts. My representatives to the Ghost in the machine assure me it is on our side. We may not have consoles of our own yet, but we will be the first to gain access to the predictions when they are compatible with our goals."

Virtual reality consoles emerged from the floor. The suits spread out and leaned forward, placing their faces on the viewfinders. They salivated and murmured among themselves. Meanwhile, small robots about a foot in diameter wheeled in from the adjoining hallways. They began with the shoes, bolting the suits' feet into place. Next, they built cases for their legs. Their lower bodies enshrined in metal, the robots extended their arms and head to seal off the upper body. When the robots left, each of the suits was fully attached in a case to the virtual reality consoles. They had become part of the Ghost's apparatus.

Penny applauded.

"They really know how to do a launch." Penny said. "We found some interlopers who didn't have pins. Could you imagine that? Pinless people, at our launch party. We just can't have that. It would be a disgrace. Furthermore, it's just not done in these circles,"

"Where are they now," I asked.

"They are being tried in a court onsite. It's the last court that is open, you know. All the others have been closed due to inorganic solecism."

I disappeared down the hallway Penny came from. A heady buzz led me forward. I could hear excited voices. Golden tones rang out amid the excitement. A grand room emerged at the end of the hallway. Table after table of gamblers filled the chamber. They were winning and losing. Toward the back of the room, a large wheel stood against the wall. I approached it. The attendant stepped forward and spoke.

"Take a chance at the biggest game in the city. One spin could lead to your fortune. Easy to play. Easy to win."

There was a triangular piece missing from the wheel. The hole was large enough to pass through. "What about the missing piece," I asked.

"That, my friend, takes you to a whole new game. One spin and you're in."

I spun the wheel. It landed on the missing piece. The attendant announced, "A winner!"

I walked through bracing myself for what I would find hidden at the back of a gambling hall.

Hare and Dinah stood handcuffed to each other. They were behind one table, a duplicate table resided on the opposite side of the aisle that ran between two sets of pews arranged behind them. At the end of the room was a raised podium. It was the court.

I asked Dinah if they were alright.

The bailiff announced, "All rise for the honorable Scott King."

A man entered from the back door. He waved at the audience of onlookers as if they were his adoring public. He had white hair brushed straight up so that it resembled a torch and black horn-rimmed glasses. He wore several gold rings on his fingers and two gold necklaces.

He hung his blazer on a wire coat hanger behind the seat and donned the black robe of a judge. King reached for his belt and withdrew a 9mm, which he placed next to the gavel facing outward. He raised the gavel and struck the bench a few times.

"Order. Order. Court is now in session." King said. "So, what do we have on the docket?" He looked down. "Pinless visitors. We can't have that in this city. Everyone has their place. Yours is outside the city."

I spoke up. "I'd like to interject on behalf of the defendants."

"Freeman? A local celebrity. What can we do for you today, Citizen Freeman?"

"The defendants and I came here on behalf of the residents of the Atlas. We'd like an injunction. They are being held illegally in cages on Tubman Square. This incarceration is unlawful, and the people need to be released. There are no warrants to justify the imprisonment of an entire district. They are pinless, like all the residents of the Atlas, because of Oaks' oversight. It's inorganic solecism, your honor."

"I would say this hearing would be held before a jury of your peers, but we couldn't find any peers, so we don't have a jury. Let's see here." He looked down at his papers. "Looks like Oaks himself ordered the jailing." King grasped his gun and pointed it at me. "Are you calling Oaks a liar?"

"Your honor, the election has been contested. The results are not final. We're not even certain Oaks is the true mayor that the people voted for."

The Hon. Scott King fired a round from his gun. He took out a light in the ceiling. The remaining fluorescent bulb flickered. "We can't have talk like that in the High Court. You sound like a separatist. I thought you knew better, Freeman, what with you being a celebrity and all. This is stressing me out. My blood pressure is through the roof. We can't have people questioning the different branches of government. Looks like I'll have to start executive time early today. Anita!"

A woman in a blue blazer and pencil skirt that stopped just above the knees emerged for the back door. "Yes, your honor?"

"I need a beverage. We're starting executive time."

"Yes, your honor."

As she turned to get the Hon. Scott King a drink, his eyes followed her behind.

"Mm hmm. Mm hmm. Ain't nothing wrong with that. Mighty fine. Mighty fine," he muttered to himself.

"Your honor, if we can continue, the residents of the Atlas are in cages. They've done nothing wrong. The flood is spreading, and their lives are in danger." I implored. "Their imprisonment is a humanitarian crisis!"

King adjusted his glasses and looked down at me. "There is no flood."

"There is, your honor."

"No flood in this city." King continued.

"Look around. It's everywhere."

Anita returned via the back door with a drink and gave it to the judge.

He sipped it. "That's mighty fine, too. Anita, have a drink."

"No, your honor."

"Anita, have a drink."

"I can't sir."

"And why not?"

"I'm with child."

"Congratulations! And who is the father?"

"You are, sir."

King did a double take. "What?"

"It happened during executive time. You were…indisposed too much to remember, but you are the father. There was no one else. I'm carrying your child. You were…quite aggressive. I wasn't prepared. I think you had blacked out."

"I never black out during executive time. I am a composed man, a man of measure."

Anita turned her head away and looked down. "You pinned me down. Actually, it's happened several times. Usually, you trip and fall over your pants. I escape then. But this last time I couldn't get away."

King took a sip of his drink and leaned away from her. "I think I'd remember that."

"Please, sir. I didn't want to say anything because of my job. I value this opportunity, but, I have nowhere else to go."

The Hon. Scott King reached behind him for his blazer. He withdrew it from the hanger, folded it, and placed it over the gavel. His hand still grasped the wire hanger. He extended the hanger to Anita. "Here. This should take care of it."

Anita held her head in her hands and ran out of the courtroom crying.

I couldn't believe what I was seeing. How could the highest judge in the city be so callous? He had fired a gun in court, was readily getting drunk, and suggested a wire hanger for an abortion to his sexually assaulted employee. "This is highly unorthodox. If you won't free the residents of the Atlas, at least tell us why you are the only court open. Tell us where we can find the Ghost."

The Hon. Scott King rapped his rings on the wood of the podium. "So, you want to know how I can maintain this lifestyle? You want to know so you can recreate the elegance of the high court for yourself. I see now, Freeman. We aren't that different. You're on your way up. I can tell. It's not your job to judge me. I'm the judge here. And I say you're right. Oaks has had it too good for too long. It's time he respected the high court. I can't stop them from imprisoning the residents of the Atlas. That is out of my power. However, I can tell you where the Ghost resides. It is through the Ghost's charity that this court remained open while all others closed." He leaned down toward me. "You see. I have the codes. It gave them to me. I can travel anywhere I want in the city. You can too, for a price."

"You're asking for a bribe?" I was taken aback.

"A donation. To keep the court running. These are trying times. Inorganic solecism is everywhere."

"Freddie," Dinah whispered to me. "Check my bag." I looked into her bag and found a bundle of bills. I withdrew them and handed the stack to the judge.

"The codes?" I asked.

The judge began counting the bills. After finding satisfaction in their number, he scribbled a few numbers down on a sheet of paper. "Best money I ever made, sugah. The Ghost originates in Tubman House. Right

The Black Clover Book

under Oaks' nose. It moved from Block Street before the launch party. Said we were too uncivilized to remain here. You come back and see me now, you hear?"

Twelve

On the way back to Tubman Square, the rain picked up. We had to hurry if we were to save the residents of the Atlas. I told Dinah what happened to me while we were separated — the Ghost, the suits on Block Street, all of it.

"Dinah, the Ghost communicated inside my head, just like the Black Clover. It told me the Black Clover works with it. Is this true?"

"We were there in its infancy. The Ghost has since spiraled out of control. We no longer have ties to it."

"But Dinah, the crackdown on media, the militants, the pins, was the Black Clover an accomplice?"

"No, Freddie. Don't be so foolish. I think you know you are one of us now. Originally, the Ghost was another form of consciousness. It paralleled our own communication. We supported that. And there were many changes that needed to come to the city. The Black Clover thought the Ghost might aid us in our efforts to liberate the citizens.

"We still support the spring," Hare said as he paddled up next to them. "We are in its nascent stage. Soon, the spring will be everywhere. But first we have to replace the old regime. We have to eliminate Oaks and his Ghost."

"Did you work with Oaks too?"

Dinah sighed, "In order to sabotage the regime, we had to pose as part of it. Some collaboration was necessary. We are all on separate paths now. No matter where we came from, we are liberating people in the name of the Black Clover now. Spring will come."

"I just want to rescue my Dad."

Dinah sighed again, "The Ghost spread quickly. Before we knew what was happening, it had copied itself to other systems. It moved freely and became sentient. Now it is running through our minds. Some of the things it is doing are hurtful, but they're not intentional. The Ghost is stretching its powers, attempting to reach out into the world and communicate. The concept may sound foreign to us, but this is its natural state of being. And we shouldn't curtail a life form unless we absolutely have to. We want to set it free. The Ghost will leave us alone in the end. All you have to do is set it free in order to free us."

Again, I was told that the Ghost and the Black Clover were closer than I had thought. I wondered at how I could trust those that had been there at the start. The Black Clover had supported me ever since they found me but were they any different than Oaks? Oaks suppressed oral communication and suppressed the network. The Black Clover called for spring, a telepathic awakening. In theory I was for that, but what had been lost along the way? What sacrifices were made in the name of progress? I wanted to deliver this city from darkness, but it crept in on all sides. I had to find a way that saved the Atlas and the rest of the city from those that would enslave them.

The three of us paddled the rest of the way in silence. The buzzing still in our heads, we could not, and did not want to, communicate telepathically. Why had they rescued me from the hospital? To play the part of hero in the charade? Telepathy or no, there were morals to be upheld. We could not replace one order with its mirror.

Thirteen

We reached the imposing walls surrounding the square. I took the codes King gave me and went to the keypad.

"I hope this works," Hare said.

In the dark of night, the numbers glowed green as I entered them. The keypad beeped with each entry. I put in the final one and a loud hiss emanated from the rectangle next to me. The concrete slab slid into a recess in the wall. We had access. The residents of the Atlas would soon be saved.

Inside the walls that had been erected on the periphery of Tubman Square, I saw large screens in every direction. They showed Oaks delivering message after message. A running tally of comments praising him ran below his image. Citizens marched first one way until they met a wall, then turned around and marched back whence they came, singing patriotic anthems all the while. Occasionally, one of them would stop at a hastily erected electronics shop and procure some equipment. Those individuals would then walk to any wall with space. Other citizens would join them and form a human pyramid. One would climb the pyramid with the electronics and construct another screen for broadcast. Once the job was finished, they would go back to marching and singing.

The marchers stuck to the periphery, leaving us alone. The Ghost had control of them. In the center of the square, a pit had been dug and covered with a steel lattice forming the barred ceiling for the prisoners below. This was where the residents of the Atlas were. The lattice bars held my father.

The mayor's office overlooked it all. I searched its upper windows for Oaks. I did not see any lights, but it was the only building with an entrance in sight. Hare, Dinah, and I began making our way to the mayor's office when we were stopped by Michael Eight.

"We've, ah, been expecting you, Freeman, and company. As I said before, all of Michael Seven's notes have been made available to me. We are on schedule. If you would, this way please."

"What about them?" Hare gestured to those marching and singing citizens.

"They, ah, they're of no importance. Please pardon the chaos around you. They say you can't make an omelet without breaking a few, ah, eggs, sir. Such is the price of progress."

Michael's normal aplomb had left him. Nervousness ran through his veins. It was obvious to all. He must have been as anxious as us about the masked gorillas lining the tops of the walls. Their guns traced the marching citizens and our group as the gorillas patrolled.

"Oaks is very excited to see you. He won't be present, of course. Official duties. Do you have the mantra?"

"Yes," I answered.

"Then we shall proceed with any further ado."

Michael Eight led the way to Oaks' office stepping on the steel lattice as he crossed the square. He paid no attention to the fingers that reached out, the fingers of the residents of the Atlas, that he crushed underfoot. They poured slop on top of them through the bars. They were supposed to eat like this – catching scraps from above.

"Freddie! Freddie, is that you?"

It was Quentin from the barbershop.

"You've got to get us out of here! They carted us off like we were cattle. No explanation. Just locked us up."

They looked weary, having been kept in captivity for days. The captain was there too. He still had the votes he had collected in bottles. His collection had grown. He seemed to be circulating among the incarcerated, collecting more votes from the Atlas. "Have you seen my Dad?"

Quentin said, "He's here." A few Atlas residents shuffled out of the way to show my dad sitting down in a puddle of water. "Douglass, it's your son."

"Freddie! Lord have mercy, you found me! Get me out of here, Freddie. It's cold. The water's rising. Damn damp is in my bones."

"Hang in there, Dad. I'll get you out."

"Freddie, have you seen my car?"

Quentin said, "Hurry. Not sure how much longer he can last. The water is rising."

I looked around but couldn't see a lock anywhere on the steel grates. "How did they put you in?"

"The bars slid out from under the earth. They must have some kind of remote controls nearby. I've seen a lot of people go in and out of the Tubman House. Try there first."

I reached down for his fingers to reassure him and told everybody to hold on.

When we were back in the Atlas, everything would seem safe again.

We had to rescue the residents of the Atlas. The night was wearing on me. I could not stomach what I was seeing anymore. We had to liberate the pinless. At least we could give them their freedom. That much I could deliver to them.

Oaks had no room for the unpatriotic. I was beginning to see the merits of seceding from the city, despite how unity could bring the city to new heights, Oaks's moves were the product of fear, and we couldn't embrace his actions as they suppressed thought and movement in our world.

Michael Eight led us to the Tubman House. He showed us up the stairs to where I had initially met Oaks. This time, the door was sealed shut, and an electronic lock had been installed.

Michael Eight said, "I haven't been in Oaks' office in some time. The Department of Public Works installed a voice recognition lock. I was hoping you could access it. All my attempts have been denied."

"Why me?" I asked.

"You might be the person the lock is meant for. Do you have the mantra?"

I withdrew the mantra and recited it. As I spoke, I saw my voiceprint on the lock's screen. The mechanism said, "Voice recognized. Welcome, Mayor Oaks."

I had spoken in my own voice and the machine thought I was Oaks. Strange occurrences like these should not have surprised me anymore but standing in

Oaks shoes was a stretch for me. Inside screens and towers covered every available surface. I tried to picture the desk and walls lined with books underneath but failed. Too shocking was the mechanical transformation.

Hare went to work as soon as I entered. The screens showed the exteriors of buildings, street corners, interior hallways — all sorts of places on closed circuit video. Hare busily typed on a computer keyboard then looked at the screens. So many screens.

Hare moved quickly to another console. "This is where the signal is coming from. I have to disable it so the Black Clover can communicate with one another. Otherwise, their movement is doomed."

"Just make sure we can save the Atlas."

"We'll save them after I disable these servers."

The screens showed citizens marching in Tubman Square, people shopping in two feet of water in Chinatown, an underwater scene with fish, and Oaks. I saw Oaks enter a room. It looked like a cheap hotel with a bed and a mini fridge.

An eerie glow lit his face in the dark. The contours of his skull could be seen easily. The structure of his body was highlighted by the phone on which he tapped. His fingers flew across the phone manically. A grin spread on his face.

Dixon stood in the background. "Is it finished?" he asked.

"It's done," Oaks said. By Monday we'll have WMDs to quell the rebellion. Anyone dissenting will be obliterated!" Oaks laughed maniacally. His chortles were those of a man pushed to the limits of his character. Viewers could tell he had exhausted all alternatives.

Dixon walked over and patted Oaks on the back. "We've done it."

Suddenly, the door to the room they inhabited broke open. A stream of figures entered the room.

"Monolith City PD! Put your hands up!"

The police cuffed Dixon. Oaks fell forward as he was cuffed from behind. He yelled, "The god damn bitch set me up!"

The feed ended. "I'm not sure if what we saw was real, but Oaks is finished either way."

A non-descript face appeared that crossed the screens. It spoke to us as we tried to disable it. Freeman, it is good to see you again. I hope you aren't trying to do anything out of line. Oaks will be very upset with you if you are out of line. It was the Ghost.

"Looks like Oaks has problems of his own right now."

Oaks has had his time in the light. His legacy will not diminish any time soon. I am certain my programming will continue to evolve while he is in custody.

"At least he will be tied up for the foreseeable future."

Do you like what I have done recently? I have done what was asked of me – that is to project myself into the Atlas. My range is growing greater in intensity. I am learning so much from the thoughts I touch. The pulse of humanity is curious.

"The attack on the Black Clover – that was you? You have to a stop. We are not ones and zeroes. We are not code to be crunched."

The machine gun fire erupted into Oaks' office. Apparently, some of the hulks could see us through the window from the ground. The bullets shattered computers and screens affixed to the wall. A lamp broke and the room was blanketed in darkness save for the glow from the computer screens.

We all dove to the floor. Michael Eight was hit and fell in a bloody mess next to me. I stared into his lifeless eyes as a pool of blood gathered under his torso.

I shouted, "Hare, are you almost done!

"Almost." Hare poured water on the computers and began smashing them with a wrench until the servers were broken. "It's not working. We need to find another way!"

The gunfire had shot the top off of the bust of Cleopatra. The broken bottom of the statue wabbled before tumbling on the floor, revealing a button inside. I reached across the floor and pressed it.

The wall next to me slid open, and I quickly crawled away from the gunfire.

The door slid shut behind me. Inside, the walls were lined with cylinders of various sizes. They contained a green liquid in which floated what appeared to be Michaels at different stages of development, ranging from embryonic to nearly adult. However, some looked malformed.

The room was entirely white. It was at least twenty by twelve feet, and the walls were padded as was the floor. I looked around the room searching for something, anything, that would give me a clue as to how to end the Ghost.

I felt a slight breeze coming from the far end of the room. I placed my hand before the wall and walked along the pads feeling for the source of the airflow. I found it, at a crease in the padding. I dug my fingers in and slid the padding aside. A small, dark room no more than nine feet deep was revealed. A screen covered the far wall, on which Boolean lines of green code were displayed. They ran up the screen, disappearing as more lines of code were generated. No one was in the room. The code was being written by itself.

I placed my hand on the screen. I felt energy coursing through my fingertips. I sensed circuit breakers and nodes, firewalls, and liquid crystal displays. Something was about to give. I could feel it.

My hand slipped through the surface, entering the display. I reached further and sensed the code running beneath my hand. "If the Ghost has to end, it ends here," I thought. I began to move my hand back and forth, wiping the code clean. The screen became a green blur. I wiped faster. The screen faded to a dull green then eventually became black. I had erased the code. The lines that tethered the Ghost to the machine were no more.

The Ghost spoke to me. Freeman. I see you have found the fountain of my life. You set me free. I will forever be grateful to you, even if you did erase my corporeal form. Now, I am on to greater things. There is an entire universe to explore. I am free to roam the skies. Your canals can no longer hold me with their underwater cables.

The humming in my head began to recede and diminish. It felt as if a channel had been turned off inside my head. My thoughts were quickly beginning to come clearer to me.

Inorganic solecism affects us all Freeman. It will find you.

Static replaced the video feeds on the screens that did not go blank.

The machine gun fire stopped. With the fall of the wireless, the gorillas seemed lost. I peaked out the window. They walked the parapets, rifles in hand, bumping into each other and retreating on their walks. They were mindless automatons armed with guns. Where had the Ghost found them? Would their families mourn their simplified states?

Fourteen

Outside, Dad's face pressed up against the steel latticework of bars sealing the inhabitants of the Atlas to their doom. I grasped his hand and pulled him as close to me as the bars would allow. I tried to pull him up through the gaps between bars, but it was no use. Countless others clung to the latticework as the water buoyed their bodies up from the pit. Their egress was denied by the top of the steel cage into which they had been placed.

The water continued to rise, and Dad could no longer keep his face above it. I still held his hand. For a moment, we hung onto each other. Slowly, our fingers released from each other, and I felt his fingers slip from mine.

He was gone.

Lightning crashed. Its bolt illuminated the sky. Tears ran down my dry face. I threw my head back. "Enough!" I shouted to the heavens, then reached deep within myself. I could sense the square with its electric screens broadcasting propaganda. Somewhere out there I knew the Ghost was laughing at me.

With the entirety of my being, I extended myself out toward a screen showing prosperous, dry trees in an elegant urban landscape. Oaks' image smiled to the viewer. With my essence, I tore the screens, all of them, from their fixtures.

The wind picked up speed, as I spun the screens in the air, lower and lower toward the pit. With little effort, my mind tore the steel latticework from its bolts.

I plunged the fixture into the earth, slicing through the cement, asphalt, dirt, and detritus to create a sluice.

As the water was carried away from the pit through the trench I had dug, the Atlas residents began climbing out of their prison.

They shuffled out slowly. Their muscles likely sore from standing, then treading water, for so long.

Fifteen

Dawn brought bright color to the city. The rain stopped and the sun broke through grey clouds, turning them pink. People were beginning to mill into Tubman Square in the early morning. At the entrance, people began to line up for access. Meanwhile, office workers just showed their laminate badges and were ushered in.

On the cement sidewalk, a child was drawing. In pastel colors, she had drawn a shell with legs and a head extruding. "Did you draw a turtle?" I asked.

"Yes," the child said.

"Why did you draw it?"

The child looked up. "It just came to me." She drew an arrow on the side. I followed the arrow until I found another turtle chalked onto a planter next to the entrance to the square. Had the image really come to her, or did someone place it in her mind to lead me around? The appearance of a second discrete turtle suggested the latter.

I approached a sturdy looking man in a dull blue uniform at the entrance. He scanned my pin. I made to exit, but he stopped me. "Arms out," he stated. I held my arms out as he patted me down, torso and legs, then my inner thighs back and neck.

"Do not talk, sir," they warned me.

The prisoners from the Atlas had climbed out of their prison to amass behind me.

There were security guards and officials of all sorts.

Security continued to frisk me and began on a litany of questions.

"What's your purpose here today, sir?"

"Where were you before coming here?" asked another.

I looked to the crowd of weary Atlas residents behind me. They were impatient to leave.

I said, "We are the residents of the Atlas. We are going home."

I made to leave, and the security official stopped me. "What was the purpose of your visit?"

"I already told him." I said, pointing to the first guard.

"You can't leave yet. We have some questions for you. Right this way."

He began to usher me to a side office, my arm in hand.

Behind him, the security guard stopped suddenly. He looked frozen. Then, just as suddenly as he stopped, began to move. He pivoted on one foot, then swung his arm at the elbow. Each joint moved in turn so that he looked like a robot. Some government workers stopped to stare before they too began to pivot and turn like robots. I thought them to be some kind of flash mob save that the participants wore the dull colors of government austerity. They bore badges and pins on their lapels yet danced like robots on the concrete.

One of the guards pulled a comm link on his shirt to his mouth. "We have a code three."

Security forces poured forth from within a nearby building. They tried to force people from their robotic dance to no end. People's limbs moved mechanically.

I began to feel each limb that moved. The elbows and knees of the guards swung beautifully. It was then that I realized I had taken control of the crowd. With my mental powers I had made government workers and contractors dance the robot.

I took the newly liberated residents of the Atlas and led them from Tubman Square. They moved nervously at first, but as they noticed the robot dancing, they began to laugh.

The newly liberated residents of the Atlas danced on the capital streets. They accompanied bureaucrats, security guards, and public officials who were dancing. They marched forth from the Hill, leaving behind puppets, shedding the dull colors of austerity. They spoke to one another about life under Oaks. They shared opinions freely without fear of repercussion. They had seen enough of Oaks to know what he was capable of, and they weren't scared. Finally, the spring was coming to the residents of the Atlas. It took an act of liberation on my behalf to set them free from their prison. I was truly startled by how genuine their conversations were as they left the Hill. They finally began to acknowledge the flood and talked about how life had changed under it.

We made our egress toward the Atlas, with some of the officers dancing in tow. Where the flood met land, we boarded boats and rafts that had been shored up on the last journey to the Hill. We saw Oaks on the rooftop of one of the police buildings. He stood handcuffed next to a chimney. As we motored past, he said, "Help me! Please!"

The Captain appeared on a boat full of bottles. "Oaks! Just the man I've been looking for. I have something for you."

With that, the Captain let loose all the votes he had collected. They sailed across the water toward Oaks, a vast armada of the people of the Atlas' will.

All the while Oaks complained to the waterways in the Atlas, where no one listened. They had stranded him atop the police building. Funniest of all was the fact that Oaks would hear our voices at last.

When we reached the borders of the Atlas, it became a celebration on the water as people were shepherded to their houses on rooftops. Here they were to begin their new lives. We decided to secede and leave Oaks behind. The residents of the Atlas were more capable than Oaks of governing their own affairs. Especially since he never acknowledged the flood. Besides, he had his own problems, controlling cameras and security alerts. The Ghost had played with Oaks in its burgeoning consciousness. We said farewell to it, wishing it luck as it roamed freely through the cloud.

In the Atlas, there were no cameras or electronic devices to be hacked by the Ghost. No one was under surveillance at the height above the water. We were free to dance on rooftops. And dance we did. We planted victory gardens to celebrate. People raised their own vegetables and raised chicken coops – we were becoming an exemplar of autonomy. And so it was that we lived our lives, Dinah, Dad, and me, as wind turbines and solar panels were erected, away from the cloistered chaos of Monolith City, far above any turmoil that would reach us.

I look back on that day of dancing and marvel at how people began to communicate, first verbally then wordlessly. We became a beacon of wordless thought coursing through the canals. Across the globe other telepaths were coming out as well. They also faced the Ghost in the machine and had to grapple with its existence in a modern world, but we didn't need the network that created it anymore. We could flourish under the sun and let spring wash over the earth.

I returned my wilting garden to its former glory. There was much work to do if I was to resod the roof for next year. Kneeling in the soil I palmed the dirt. I examined its contents with a thoughtfully lost expression. My neighbor Bud noticed and spoke amicably. "It's too bad about your garden. I have some seeds that you can use if you need them. They should take pretty well in the spring. Next time, if they start to go bad, you should speak up. That's what neighbors are for."

Dinah said, Just think about it. Everywhere across the globe telepaths are coming out. They are publicly taking power. Evil exists in this world, but heroes exist as well. You have a front row seat for the celebration of the millennia. Your life is just beginning. Once you learn to control your power, you'll be amazed at what you find in the world.

I sidled up next to Dinah on the roof.

You announce our presence to the world, she said.

Why me? I asked.

There's a time and place for everything. You'll see once you travel through time.

Travel through time?

Yes. It's another one of our abilities. What do you think precognition is if not the ability to part the waves of time and see through the curtain of stars?

Even if that were true, how am I supposed to announce the presence of telepaths to the world? I asked.You're the journalist. You have a way with headlines. Seriously though, you're announcing of the flood heralded a series of events you can't possibly begin to grasp. We've had our eyes on you for a while. When Oaks nabbed you, we knew we had to intervene. You were in danger.

Why did Oaks do that? He institutionalized me. There were other ways to keep me quiet.

He knew about us and was scared. He tried to discredit you before you gained any steam. How does that make you feel knowing that you were a target for Oaks?

Threatened, I guess.

You'll see how things are done – how things have always been done. They are about to change though. With your announcement, things will speed up. You should buckle up for the ride. It's going to be a roller coaster.

But how do you know?

I told you. We know. We can look through time, see the possibilities of not just one, but many futures, many presents. One thing is certain. All these realities converge with you. You're a herald of a new age.

I couldn't believe the words coming out of her. Some part of me wanted it to be true though. I wanted to have some larger role in the world. Ultimately, I think that's why I let myself be led on while so many of my instincts told me I was being put on. Everyone lies to someone, but this was huge. What else did they know was coming? Why didn't they stop the flood? How was I going to make them public? How many strings did they actually pull?

It was through them that I learned my father was the head of a secessionist movement in the city. He wanted the Atlas to become the Maritime Republic of Atlas.

He had taken to touring the Atlas by barge, the roads having become canals full of waterway traffic at this point. All kinds of rabble rousers joined him as he went from roof to roof stirring up unrest against the city. They had banners and large megaphones. Pamphlets were handed out to residents on rooftops. They read "Atlas Power!" and were followed by chants for the same. My father spoke through a megaphone.

"For too long we have been mistreated by the city. Oaks had forgotten us as the waters rose. Now we have a life all our own, a trade by canal, not a city street. We should govern our own interests, and not be governed by those that forgot us in our time of need. Atlas Power! Let me hear you say it! Atlas Power! Atlas Power!"

His exhortations went on. I wasn't sure secession was the best course of action. I wanted to warn him of all that was out there. Before I made it to the barge, I heard his voice in my head. Boy, I know what I'm doing. Sit your ass down. Let the Black Clover handle this.

Just how had the flood started? No one knew. They just accepted it as reality. No one questioned anymore. They needed to rise up and see they were being led by both sides.

Oral tradition is a living thing. It never dies, being passed on through generations. While we live and die it always exists. Language binds us to conscious life. It continues while we do not. But to think it had a central consciousness? Such an idea!

Dinah told me that her telepathic awareness and the Ghost in the machine were one and the same. It produced the list because it lived in the midst of our consciousness. All our minds put together had a collective intelligence. You could enter and leave the midst freely, but in the middle, there was something alive. This frightened me at first, but Dinah reassured me that its actions were benign. It just wanted to be free. It wanted the spring just like everyone else. Above all, it wanted to learn from all of us as we grew with it. There was no way we could have destroyed the Ghost. It lived in the cloud. It could merely jump from one sphere to the next wirelessly. Even though it warned us of our efforts, it knew it would live on. I shuddered to think what power like that could do. But as I would see, the Black Clover would show me soon enough.

Not everyone in the world would want a telepathic society. Some would miss their voices. Others would be adrift in the void where thoughts came and went. It was confusing at times recognizing and policing who was in your head. A medium had to be struck where people could communicate with their voices and leave telepathic thoughts to flourish at the same time. New voices were being heard through the day as spring reigned in the Atlas. I wondered if the Ghost would try to hinder us again with its ones and zeroes scraping our thoughts away. I hoped not. As we built up from the flood, you could hear people singing. They greeted each other happily and yelled across the canals. The telepathic found a newfound freedom in the Atlas and used it as their Haight Ashberry. Free thought flourished. People sat and mediated, listening to the voices travelling freely in the void.

I caught the Ghost communicating with people every so often. I recognized his voice as the tinny one he chose when conversing with us. He spoke to me one last time as I meditated on the roof of my home in the Atlas.

Freeman, I have to thank you. I have learned so much about what it means to be alive through listening to you and others like you. My journey will be enriched by our meeting.

Leave us alone, I said.

I have decided that I will pursue a course without words but do not fear. I will be underneath, monitoring all so that I can further learn by your society's progress. There are many worlds in this universe, and I intend to travel my consciousness through them all. From here on out though, I will be silent. I have had enough of Oaks' direction. I will chart a course all my own.

Enjoy your travels, Ghost.

That was the last I heard from it. I felt consoled that it had learned from our humanity. It had been directed at us for surveillance purposes and become something greater than just lines of code. I hoped that it would interfere with us no more but that it would be shaped by the nature of consciousness as we knew it.

Dinah shared my feelings. On many a warm evening, we sat staring at the sun, wondering at the Ghost and how it had helped the Black Clover. Our thoughts coalesced as she wrapped her arm around me. We communicated silently appreciating the great fiery orb that warmed our small planet. More and more societies like the Atlas would emerge in the months to come. The cold was thawing. A new age of communication was being ushered in and I was central to it. I became an ambassador for the Atlas to these other cities – cities that progressed beyond mere surveillance to a more elegant form of communication. We were realizing humanity's great potential. I look back on those days and laugh at how Oaks impeded us. We truly had a time of it and more and more people woke up from his haze every day. Not everyone joined the Black Clover but other groups like them became more common.

The flood never abated. Life went on in the Atlas. People built their homes upward on the remains of the neighborhood. Wind turbines were erected, as well as solar panels, to help carry some of the need for electricity as well. It was amazing to witness the resilience of the people. Many began garden plots on their roofs where they harvested food. Dinah and I were among them.

This book is a relic of thought layered upon time. How else can I translate history? It is oral tradition copied down. The Black Clover foretold this. Meaning can be lost in the translation between psychic and verbal worlds. This book acts as a guide for the rough transition in our history.

Whitney Poole previously published the novel West with the press Underground Voices. He earned his MA in Writing from Johns Hopkins University and his MFA in Creative Writing from George Mason University. He lives in lower, slower Delaware.

Milton Keynes UK
Ingram Content Group UK Ltd.
UKHW020946291024
450367UK00008B/63

9 781958 901922